Solitude

An NZ Series

Joseph L. Wilder, MPA

Dedications

To my college professor, Lynne Murray, who saw the writer in me. Many years ago, she encouraged me to write.

To the love of my life, Tamara, who was frustrated by my countless hours spent with the computer, but refrained from complaining. Thank you for the support. I love you.

To my children: Noah, thank you for your undying excitement for my stories. You offer insight and ideas that keep me typing. Sydney Rose, welcome to the world. You are not allowed to read this book until you are 10, put it back on the shelf ☺. You are both loved very much, and bring immense joy into our lives.

To my nieces and nephews (all 20-something of you)! I hope you enjoy this and never stop reading.

Reading = Knowledge. Knowledge = Power. Power = Success.

Most of all, I dedicate this creation to Him that has blessed me with talent, inspiration, and creativity. He that has allowed me to bounce ideas off and has gifted me with ideas via dreams. My eternal confidant, the Maker and Creator of all things - God.

Finally, to the readers: may you all enjoy this as much as I have enjoyed the writing.

ENJOY!

INTRODUCTION

Various people struggle to come to terms with their inexplicable change in appetites. Relationships deteriorate as loved ones fall victim to the changes. Grocery stores struggle to meet the demand. Neighborhoods and cities quickly decline.

At the threshold of total anarchy, local authorities feverishly attempt to maintain order as people and pets go missing. A race against the clock, Sheriff Glasgow pulls out all the stops in attempts to serve and protect the people of his San Francisco East Bay County.

World health organizations battle with a new viral outbreak. Laboratories work around the clock trying to develop a vaccine.

With the origins of the new virus unknown, President Riley, of the United States, attempts to determine if his country inadvertently developed the strain. The US government may possess the cure to the apocalyptic virus, but to share this knowledge would be to compromise national security. The President worries about exposing too much to the world about what the Americans have been brewing behind closed doors.

The first book and introduction of the NZ series. A new twist to the stale apocalyptic stories. Solitude introduces a realistic end of days scenario that will capture readers and have them begging for another serving.

Chapter 1

Malcolm ran down the main boulevard at 3:30 in the morning. A ritual of sorts that he had performed since he was an eleven year-old training for the wrestling team. Now he was a lean 43-year-old man. He loved running at night, when everyone was sleeping, the bars were empty, and the streets were vacant. He ran with his iPod blaring Chromeo into his eardrums, his feet hitting the pavement to the thumping of the hypnotic dance beat.

He had enjoyed running since he was a boy. He first fell in love with the sport by running with his father. He loved to run mostly in the wee hours of the morning when nobody was awake. Running down the middle of major boulevards absent of traffic was freeing. Sometimes he would allow his mind to wander and pretend he was running fast enough to justify his presence in the 40-mile per hour lanes.

This was one of the places and times when he found Solitude. Malcolm found more religious satisfaction through his nightly runs than he ever did in a church. He prayed and meditated on his runs. His mind always cleared while running, and he was able to think through anything that weighed his mind down. Tonight was especially troubling.

Malcolm knew his cravings were becoming dangerous. He and his wife, Brenda, had always been completely open with each other. He shared with her his feelings when the cravings began. But Malcolm failed to share with her the details of his late night outings.

The early morning runs had morphed into late night hunting and feeding expeditions. His prey began innocently with road kill. Embarrassed of his thoughts and drive, he carefully made sure that no one was around before dragging a cat into the bushes that lined Grimmer Blvd. There he devoured the animal as if he had been naturally doing so all his life. He felt embarrassed and ashamed. He cleaned himself as best he could in the flood canal before running home. Now that night seemed so long ago, almost as if it were another life altogether. He had since then graduated to stealing dogs from neighbors' yards.

Chapter 2

The dreams began sometime ago. Jack remembered the first time he had the dream – it was so vivid. Like any dream, the emotions he felt communicated more than the visual properties.

In the dream, he had an insatiable hunger. He walked a far distance, what seemed like days, following the scent. He wondered if it was a BBQ he smelled. The scent was so powerful, overwhelming, and desirable. He never felt a greater desire to consume meat.

The dream did not make sense. He was able to smell the meat from miles away. In the dreams, he never was able to satisfy the hunger. Upon waking, he could never recall ever finding the source of the scent.

Upon waking, his pillow would be drenched in drool that had trickled from his mouth and down his cheek. The side of his face displayed a white crusty line depicting the path the saliva travelled.

The searching for meat dreams continued, each time it seemed that his sense of smell and his desire for the meat increased. It never seemed that he was ever able to acquire the intended carnivorous feast.

To combat the unsatisfying dreams, he found himself daydreaming of eating steaks, burgers, filet mignon, and meat loaf. He would fall asleep imagining the Thanksgiving style feast of a table full of meat. His nightly meditative ritual turned into a mental smorgasbord of omnivorous proportions. Each night he would fall asleep willing his dreams to end in an award finding of a Brazilian churrasco.

Jack's wife, Tessy, was the love of his life. She began accusing him of sleep eating. Jack defensively did not believe her, so she videotaped him.

There in vivid color was the proof. Jack appeared to be awake while he raided the fridge in his sleep. They were both disgusted as they watched Jack tear apart raw packages of bloody ground beef, and devour everything that had a hint of a meaty smell.

Strangely, after the raid, Jack would clean up after himself. In his sleep, he covered his tracks; wiping down the fridge, cleaning up the bloody mess that accumulated on the floor and counter, and cleaned up his face. Then he returned to bed as if nothing out of the ordinary had transpired.

They discussed seeking help, but whom should they call? He was not ill, was not hurting himself or anyone else, everything else was normal.

Tessy was sharing the disturbing nocturnal behavior with her best friend via Facebook. Jennifer, a dietician and social worker for Alameda County, suggested that he might be lacking protein or iron in his diet. Tessy agreed to supply iron supplements and increase the meat in Jack's diet. While sleep behaviors fascinated Jennifer, they freaked-out Tessy.

Chapter 3

That night, Tessy presented Jack with a spaghetti dinner that consisted of more ground beef and meatballs than the stringy noodles. Jack looked longingly at his wife and tried to express his gratitude for her loving support. He ate the meal graciously and allowed her to believe that there was a chance that it might work.

Jack knew that the cooked meat would not satisfy this new found craving. The craving was not just for meat; it seemed to be specifically for raw meat. He had trouble sourcing the cause for the craving, but he knew it was true.

Jack had always loved eating meat, except for the short rebellious period in High School when he made an attempt at being vegetarian. That stance was a poor attempt at gaining the attention of a pretty girl. What the experience made him realize was that all of his favorite meals contained meat.

After depriving himself for a few weeks, he finally caved when his mother ordered a *Meat Lover's* pizza for dinner. Now looking back at this memory, Jack could not recall who the girl was - that momentarily altered his life - but he could still remember the smell of that pizza. His mouth watered each time he recalled the memory.

Chapter 4

Having run further than usual, Malcolm was covered in sweat. He continued to run in search of something to eat. He found it strange, there was no road kill, no wandering strays, no raccoons in the dumpsters behind the grocery stores, and no possums crawling up from the storm drains.

Driven solely by his desire to feed, Malcolm did not register the cramping in his legs. His calves and thighs begged for a rest. His pace had slowed tremendously, but he continued to run. His lungs burned with each intake of the nearly frozen air. His exhalations made him appear as a human steam-locomotive making his way down the country highway.

He stopped running in his suburban neighborhoods long ago to avoid the chance of a neighbor finding him gnawing on their precious *Fluffy*. The change to the country highway was a perfect decision. The highway was a gold mine of road kill. Malcolm often feasted on deer, raccoons, and dogs. It was a slow night if he could only find a squirrel or two. But tonight, there was nothing.

Malcolm decided it was time to head back home when the rain began to fall. He looked up at the sky and detested the rain gods for interrupting his hunt. After shaking his fist at the darkened sky, he turned around to head back homeward.

When he turned he saw the approaching headlights of a vehicle coming around the bend. The headlight illuminated a grove of Coyote Brush about 20 yards from the road. It was in the lights of the vehicle that he caught a glimpse of a human body in the bushes.

After allowing the vehicle to pass, Malcolm ran across the road and approached the bush where he had seen the body. Sure enough, there was the backside of a human. He was wearing jeans and a black windbreaker. The body was soaked from the rain.

Malcolm cautiously approached, wondering if the guy was dead. Immediately, the thought of satisfying his hunger with the possible corpse entered his mind. Malcolm noticed that his mouth was watering and he slurped his saliva back into his mouth and swallowed. He wiped his mouth with the sleeve of his running jacket. Just then the mass in the bushes shifted. It appeared as if the body had gone instantly stiff. The hair on the back of Malcolm's neck stood up as he waited to see if he had imagined the movement.

Risking an altercation, Malcolm called out, "Hello! Hey, are you ok?"

The mass spun around quickly to face Malcolm. He was crouched in a wrestler's stance. The sight took Malcolm aback. The man's face was dripping with blood. His lips were pulled back, baring his teeth. Blood drooled out of his mouth and it sounded like the man both growling and hissing.

Chapter 5

Malcolm strained to see the bloody mass that the man had been feasting on. It was such a bloody massacre that he could not tell what kind of animal it was.

"Hey man, it's cool, no worries. I'm not going to take your meal."

Malcolm was trying to calm the situation down before he became the man's second course for the night. He slowly reached into his pocket and pulled out the pack of body wipes he carried for cleaning up after his feastings. He slowly held out the pack as a peace offering to the snarling, bloodied man.

"Here, do you need some wipes to clean up?"

The man continued to snarl, his eyes locked on Malcolm's. It seemed that he was daring Malcolm to make a move. Malcolm was not sure what to do next. Should he move toward the guy, slowly back away, turn and run. He was afraid that any movement would cause the guy to pounce. In all his dealings with wildlife, he was not sure how this related. Bears, mountain lions, and dogs make yourself large and make lots of noise. For snakes, move slowly away, avoiding any sudden movements. But Malcolm was unsure how to react to a human predator. He began to wonder if he could put up a good enough fight to take the person. Under normal circumstances, he felt he had a good chance, but this person appeared to be crazed.

Malcolm again invited for the man to take the package of wipes. It was obvious the man wanted nothing to do with the wipes. Malcolm resolved to slowly placing the wipes on the ground and slowly backed away from the situation. He continued to back up until he felt the asphalt under his running shoes. There he stopped and continued to watch the man. The man remained in his crouched position, softly snarling, eyes still locked.

Malcolm became flooded with light, a horn blared, he jumped off the road tumbling in the dirt. The tires screeched as the car spun onto the shoulder. The headlights circling into the night sky like a searchlight. Malcolm jumped up; the guy in the bush was gone.

The driver jumped out his car. Relieved to see Malcolm up and walking he began to yell, "What the hell are you doing standing in the middle of the highway at three in the morning? Are you trying to get yourself killed?"

Malcolm couldn't believe the guy was yelling at him. He was the one speeding around corners like a maniac.

Malcolm decided to take the higher road and held up his hands, "I'm sorry man. I was just out here jogging. Are you alright?"

"Yea, I'm alright, but you are going to get killed. You are not even wearing reflective clothing, what is wrong with you? And who runs at 3:00 in the morning?"

Malcolm was now close enough that he could smell alcohol hanging on the driver's breath. He took notice that the front of the man's shirt was soaked as well as his lap.

"Wait a minute, have you been drinking?" Malcolm accused.

"F-off prick," the man yelled as he jumped back into his car and pressed on the gas. "Stay off the road, jogger-boy." With that the car kicked out dirt and gravel and the guy continued on his way.

Malcolm returned his gaze to the bush. He wondered if the guy had run off or was nearby waiting to return to his meal. He wanted to check out the corpse to see if it were human or animal and if there was anything left to ward off his hunger. He looked around and saw nobody around. His adrenaline was still pumping, his senses aware. He was dumbfounded that he saw somebody else, feeding in the middle of the night. He decided that he should not risk his luck any further this evening. He walked back onto the road and began running toward home, still hungry.

Chapter 6

Dillon Keller, by all accounts, was a hothead. He was born and raised in the Parks neighborhood. Everyone knew him and his family. People either loved or hated the Kellers.

His pops was the original owner of their four-bedroom – two bath tract home. His father, a Vietnam vet, intentionally purchased the home in the all-white subdivision in 1966. He was sorely distraught when – shortly after moving in – the Fair Housing Act of 1968 was passed. Even so, it wasn't until a decade later, that minorities began taking up residence in the Parks.

Dillon, the youngest of three, grew up attending public school - where whites had become the minority. He did not share the same racist opinions of his father, but after repeated run-ins with gangs like the Nortenos, X13, Asian Persuasion, and the Afgani gang "SAG"; Dillon was turning more and more into his father.

Unable to go to college - 'on account of being too white' - Dillon followed in his father's footsteps and joined the Marines. After serving multiple tours in both Iraqi wars and Afghanistan, he went to work at the machine shop with his father. He was on his way to purchasing a home and moving out, when the shop closed. Unable to find replacement work, he continued to live at his parents' house.

Dillon had packed heat since he was 14, after a serious beating he received. He was on the wrestling team, visiting a neighboring high school for a match, he was jumped on his way between the locker room and the gym.

He had left the event to use the restroom. On his way back, members of X13 jumped him. They confronted him for wearing the wrong color, even though the only thing he had on was his blue wrestling singlet.

They called him a white-honkey-Nazi as they wailed on his crouched body. Three Mexicans kicked him in his gut and head before running off. His wrestling team found him bloodied and unconscious on the cold pavement.

From that point on, Dillon always packed heat. He purchased a small 9 mm that a White Supremist gave him a great deal on. He paid $50 for the gun. The guy warned him to never get caught with the gun.

"It comes with a history, that's all I'm saying," he had said. "If you ever tell where you got this, it's gonna be your family that pays the price. Got it?"

Dillon carried the gun with him everywhere, but he had never had to use it. Instead, he took up boxing and began fighting his opponents. Knowing he had his 9 mm backup gave him the confidence to win the fights.

On his 18th birthday, his father handed down to him a .45 Winchester Magnum. It was this gun that he used to defend his neighborhood on the night that his Afghan neighbors brought trouble to his street.

The Afghans moved in across the street several years back. This made Dillon's father's blood boil. The situation became even worse when they realized that the two boys in the family were heavily involved in an Afghan gang.

To make matters worse, a wannabe-gang-banger, lived around the corner. The Mexican kid and his friends were trying to make a name for themselves – taking it upon themselves to 'deal' with the Afghans.

It was about 11:30 at night on a cold, fall evening. Dillon, and his buddy Paul, had just walked home from Raliegh's Pub. They were standing on his parent's driveway on Ravensbourne Street, smoking unfiltered Camel cigarettes before parting for the night.

Two of the Mexican kids went walking by. A silver Audi with tinted windows was coming up the street. Nothing unusual to cause alarm until the car's window rolled down and the sound of an accelerated engine filled the air.

The car sped by as the passenger opened fire on the Mexican's. Dillon dropped to the ground behind his truck. Within seconds, it was all over. Dillon lifted his head as the silver Audi sped away. He saw the two Mexicans sprawled on the sidewalk, not moving.

He looked over to Paul who was holding his upper arm. He moved over to him.

"You alright? You hit?"

"Yeah, the bastards shot my arm!"

"Come on, get in my truck, I'll get you to the hospital."

The guys jumped in Dillon's truck and pulled out into the street.

Paul said, "those guys took a left. They'll have to take Everglades to get out of the neighborhood. You know they'll be heading straight for 880. We can go down Isle Royal and head them off at Yellowstone."

"What about your arm?"

"I'll live, it only grazed me. Let's get those bastards!"

"Getti-up!"

Chapter 7

Jack and Tessy habitually did their grocery shopping together every Sunday evening. It usually was uneventful but they enjoyed the time together. They strolled the aisles together and occasionally ran into familiar faces. They knew the store clerks by name. This Sunday, the tradition took on an unfamiliar turn of events.

Like usual, Jack assumed the responsibility of choosing the meat for the week. With his new developed 'taste' for meat, it was taking more of their shopping time and budget. So Tessy resolved to leave Jack in the meat department while she continued with the shopping.

Typically, Jack would catch up to her with his selections and they would finish shopping together. Now, as Tessy stood at the front of the store waiting for him, she wondered what was going on. She pulled out her phone and quick-dialed Jack. As the call went through, a commotion broke out and screams for help filled the air from one end of the store.

Chapter 8

Jack knew his problem was getting out of hand. He tried to keep most of the details from Tessy, but he was troubled by this fascination. He dutifully ate her cooked meals in attempts to please her, but secretly he would sneak bites of raw meat from the fridge.

Now as he stood in the meat department, his mouth began to salivate. He stood there mesmerized by one particular package. There on top of a stack of prepackaged cellophane encased portions of beef, sat a family sized portion of blood enriched London Broil.

It is not unusual for blood to seep through the cellophane of wrapped meat. Tessy insisted that Jack bag all of the meat separately before adding the items to the shopping cart. For some unidentifiable reason, this package had Jack mesmerized.

He stood there in a stupor and watched the blood drip off the package and down into a small forming puddle on the floor. Jack could faintly register the music the store had playing. It was muffled in the background of his thoughts, back there with the other cacophony sounds of the store. The sounds only seemed to be registering on a subconscious level. His full awareness was concentrating on the dripping of the red liquid. As if someone had taken control of his mind and body. He wondered if he was having an out-of-body experience, but quickly decided otherwise being that he was still in his body. The next things he recalled were the screams.

Chapter 9

Dillon floored the accelerator. The back tires of his Chevy Silverado laid two long lines of rubber from his house to the corner. The same tires squealed as Dillon took a hard right-turn onto Isle Royal. Paul winced in pain, trying his best to tie a torn shirt around his wounded arm.

They sped up, hitting 50 miles an hour. The homes and parked cars along the road became a blur. Dillon kept his truck in the middle of the road, praying that nobody would pull out into his path.

Two cats in chase ran out in front of them. With no time to react, Dillon flew over both of them. The guys felt the cats bump up against the undercarriage of the truck. Paul spun around in his seat to see one of the cats tumble several feet into the air before dropping on the asphalt.

The guys looked at each other, but did not slow the vehicle. They reached the four-way stop at the intersection of Isle Royal and Yellowstone. Dillon spun his truck around and positioned his truck at the stop sign on Yellowstone.

"You take your side of the street," Dillon said while handing the 9 mm to Paul.

They jumped out of the cab and took cover behind parked vehicles.

Just as they had begun to wonder if the Afghans had beat them, or taken a different direction, the silver Audi came racing up the street.

The car slowed behind the truck that was idling at the stop sign. They laid on the horn, attempting to get the truck to move.

Then Dillon popped up from behind the green Honda Civic and fired 3 bullets into the driver's side window, instantly killing the driver with a headshot.

Paul followed suit, popping up and advancing on the passenger from behind. He unloaded all 7 of the bullets in his clip.

Dillon jumped up on the hood of the Audi and unloaded the rest of his clip through the windshield.

The guys then drove to Baylands and down a dirt road to the Leslie Salt pond marshes. They walked out on the wooden planks that ran for miles into the San Francisco Bay. They ditched both of the guns into the stinky mud of the Mowry Slough, exposed from the low tide. The guns disappeared into the muck. Come high tide, the guns would sink deeper, never to be seen again.

Back at the truck, Dillon looked at Paul's arm.

"It probably needs stitching."

"Forget it, we can't go to the hospital now! We might as well just drive straight to the police station and confess. No way! Take me to Sahara."

Dillon drove Paul back to Raliegh's, where the crazy night had begun. The pub was closed, but Sahara was still inside cleaning and stocking. Dillon called from his cell.

"Hey, we need your help, open the back door would ya?"

Seconds later, the back door flew open. Sahara ushered the two in, glancing around the back alley before closing the door.

"What the hell is going on? What happened?" Sahara questioned.

"Crazy Afghan drive-by. They got Paul in the arm."

"Holy Shit! Why are you here instead of the hospital?"

"We can't go to the hospital, please 'don't ask, don't tell.'"

Sahara's gaze locked on Dillon's. She understood, and did not want to know anything else.

"Ok, Paul, go into the back room." Sahara yelled as she headed to fetch the Bar's first-aid kit.

She returned to the back and told Paul to remove his shirt. The side of his shirt was bloodied.

"Go wash this out in the sink," She ordered Dillon.

Then she went about examining the wound.

"This is nothing, you big baby. It only grazed you."

"You haven't heard me wine about it, have you?"

Paul winced as Sahara poured hydrogen peroxide on the wound.

She then scrubbed at the wound with a clean towel. She filled the wound with Neosporin before securing the skin closed with three butterfly bandages.

"There you go tough guy."

The three of them sat in the bar for the next few hours, taking shots and waiting for the heat to die down. Dillon left his truck at the bar for the next few days, just to be safe.

Neither one of them were ever suspected or even questioned.

Chapter 10

Brenda realized that something was changing in her husband Malcolm. He typically would go running in the middle of the night, that was nothing new. But where his runs use to be for an hour, now they were lasting several hours. She never took her man for one who would cheat on her, but she wondered what was going on.

His demeanor had changed. He seemed tired, his face was going pale, becoming sunken, and his eyes were dark and sunken. She questioned him if he was feeling ok, he stated that he was fine and to not worry. She gave him the distance he requested, that was until she found the blood on his clothes.

It was not unusual for Malcolm to return from his early morning run and throw his clothes straight into the washer. Brenda often would transfer the laundry into the dryer later in the morning. It was a ritual that they had formed over the course of their relationship. When Brenda pulled Malcolm's clothes out this morning, the blood stained jogging jacket concerned her.

Chapter 11

His lovely wife usually greeted Malcolm at the door. When he arrived home from work; she typically greeted him with a kiss and a mixed drink. Today was different; nobody was there as he entered the house.

"Hello, Honey, I'm home," Malcolm yelled out.

After no response he turned the corner into the kitchen. He stopped abruptly when he saw his wife standing in the kitchen with her arms behind her.

She slowly asked, "Are you ok, did you hurt yourself?"

He looked at her puzzled and stumbled with his words.

She repeated, "Are _ you _ ok, _ did _ you _ hurt _ yourself?"

He finally formed the words, "Babe, what do you mean? Why are you talking like this?"

Brenda then pulled out his blood stained jacket. She inquired, "What did you do, WHAT DID YOU DO?"

Malcolm pleaded, "Honey please, sit down…"

Brenda's voice raised and quacked, "I don't want to sit down, I want you to explain why there is blood on your jacket! Did you hurt somebody? There is a lot of blood here and you don't seem to be injured at all, so, who did you hurt? What is going on with you? You were gone for several hours this morning and then your jacket turns up all bloody and you never offer me an explanation? What the hell is going on?"

Malcolm had never lied to his wife; sure he had avoided sharing information at times, but never out right lied to her. That afternoon he felt that he had no choice. They promised to stick by each other forever, no matter what. They would never turn on each other, never give up on each other, but that was before he took up the practice of eating roadside decaying meat and their neighbor's pets.

Each morning he had rinsed off his running jacket. It was Gore-Tex and made for a great shield from the blood and rinsed off easily. He hadn't realized that the blood had dripped down his chin and neck and ran inside his jacket. The inside liner was white, making the red stain pop and impossible to ignore.

Malcolm began fabricating his story on the fly, amazed with how easy it was to lie to his wife. He actually felt himself believing the story.

"I was running along the highway and I tripped on a dead dear that I hadn't seen. After I picked myself up off of the ground, I went back to the deer. She was still alive and whining in pain. I didn't know what else to do, so I picked up a boulder and… well you know…"

He shrugged his shoulders and looked down at the ground.

"I didn't know what else to do, Babe."

"OH MY GOSH," Brenda let out.

She crossed the room and gave him a hug. She had bought the lie and Malcolm sighed in relief. He would have to be more careful from this point on.

Chapter 12

"I am not b-s'n you. People's pets are disappearing. Animal control is saying that they are responding to more than usual call outs for dead animal recoveries. At first the authorities thought that there might be a mountain lion again. But the attacks are too wide spread and numerous" Dillon attempted to convince his drinking buddies.

"What are you suggesting, that there is a serial 'pet-killer' on the loose?" Paul inquired. The group began laughing, all of them except Dillon.

The group of young men met for drinks every night after work. This became a ritual shortly after high school. Before they were old enough to enter the bars, the guys would gather in parking lots, under highway overpasses, or at the end of a road. They would hang out for a couple of hours before heading home. Now they always ended up at Raliegh's Pub. A small bar, but it had a dartboard, a pool table, and Sahara was the bartender.

Sahara was of Scottish descent and it was evident. She was stocky, had red-curly locks of hair, and light freckles splattered on her pale skin. She had the temperament that took no monkey business from anyone.

Sahara had been part of the group since she could drive. She was a couple of years older than the guys and as soon as she obtained her license, she became the designated driver for the group. They spent countless nights cruising in her white convertible 1978 VW Beetle. She got pregnant and gave birth her senior year. She began working nights at Raliegh's as soon as she was old enough. Now she was the head bartender and literally ran the joint.

"I don't know what is happening, but it ain't no mountain lion," Dillon responded.

"Hey guys, it is true. Nick's beagle went missing about a week ago" Sahara chimed in as she wiped down the bar.

"Oh come on, that damn dog was always running away. It could have gotten hit by a car or found a better life and decided not to come back," Gregory added.

"Yea, well all I know is that a bunch of men are getting together and organizing a patrol to try and catch whoever is doing this," Dillon continued. "I'm planning on joining them."

"What do they think they are going to find?" Gregory asked.

"Who knows, but when they do, that dude ain't going to see his next sunrise and I wanna be apart of that action" Dillon concluded.

The rest of the men nodded in agreement. Paul suggested that they do their own patrolling to increase their chances of finding the perp. The others agreed. They planned to head home, grab weapons, and dress for the night. At 11 pm, they would convene at Raliegh's, down a shot and head out on patrol.

Chapter 13

Seth Parker had just finished a meeting and was on his way to the Pete's Coffee down the street. His phone buzzed in his pocket. He looked at the screen to see his wife's name on the display. He slid his finger across the screen to accept the call.

"Hey Babe, just on my way to grab some coffee, what's going on?"

"Seth!"

His wife's voice was shaky and quiet.

"Honey, what is it? What's going on?"

"There's a man in the house."

"What? Have you called the police?"

"No, I'm so scared. I grabbed the kids and ran into our closet. I panicked and all I could think was to call you."

Seth quickly scrolled through his contact list, located the dispatch number for the local police department and opened a conference call. This was the only time that he was grateful for his rowdy neighbors that caused him to save the dispatch number.

"Babe, did you grab your gun?"

Seth and Cammie had purchased handguns and practiced together on a monthly basis. Cammie insisted that the only way she would allow Seth to give her a gun is if he trained her on how to use it safely and if it was a pink. So they purchased a Pink Lady Smith & Wesson.

"No, I am so sorry. I panicked. Now I'm too scared, I don't know where he is."

Seth never understood why people run and hide in closets. There is no escape, and the doors never have locks. He wondered if it stemmed back to childhood or even the womb. Closets were favorite hiding places for children. They were small, closed in, and comfortable. Plus, there were lots of things to hide behind.

"It's ok, Cam, it is ok. We'll figure something out."

"911 dispatch, what's your emergency?"

"Hello, Hi. My name is Seth Parker. My wife is on the line; we are conferenced in. She is at home with our children and says there is an intruder. They are hiding in a closet. Please send the police to 323 Waterview Terrace right away."

Chapter 14

"Ok, Mrs. Parker? Can you hear me?"

The sound of the dispatcher's voice was reassuring and Cammie's heartbeat settled.

"Yes, I am here. Please hurry."

"Mrs. Parker, the police are on their way. Please remain calm. I am going to stay on the line until you are safe, okay?"

"Alright."

Seth interrupted, "Honey, do you have your Bluetooth?"

"Yes, yes, it is in my pocket."

"Put the Bluetooth on and listen to me."

The operator and Seth both had to hold their earpieces away from their ears as they heard the brushing sounds of Cammie retrieving her device from her pocket.

"Okay, it is on."

"Alright, get the kids to the back of the closet and cover them up. Tell them to cover their ears and close their eyes."

Both Seth and the operator could hear Cammie shuffling and whispering the instructions to their two kids.

"Ok, now what?"

"Ok, now, on my side of the closet, on the shelf, behind the boxes, I have my old shotgun. Be careful, it is loaded. Quietly pull it out."

Again, they could hear Cammie as she labored to remain silent. They could hear her heavy breathing. Each time she moved a box, she held her breath and then slowly released it.

"Oh my gosh, I can hear him, he's coming down the hall!"

"That's okay. Stay focused. Get the gun down, take it off of safety."

"Honey, I don't know how to shoot a shotgun. I have only shot my gun before."

"I know, I know. But it is easy and I'm going to walk you through it. Now, do you have the gun?"

"Yes, I have it."

"Take the safety off..."

"Where's the safety?"

"Near the trigger, just like your gun."

"Ok, got it."

"Now, grab the lower part of the barrel with your left hand and pull it back until it clicks and then slide it forward again."

They could hear the unmistakable telltale sound of the shotgun sliding a shell into the chamber. If the perpetrator was within earshot, he either crapped his pants or high tailed it out of there.

"Okay, good. Now put the butt end of the gun up tight against your shoulder and point the gun at the door. Get a good shooting stance and aim for his belly. The gun is going to give a good kick, so get ready."

"Seth, I can't do this. I can't shoot anyone. I'm so scared."

"Cam-honey, listen to me. It is either him or our babies. You have to shoot him to protect our little ones. Don't you dare let him get you or the kids. Do you hear me? You do what you have to do to protect yourselves. You can do this. Do not think of him as a human being, he is a monster. A monster wants to kill you and the kids! Shoot the monster! You can do this!"

They could hear the muffled sounds of crying. Seth could picture his wife, standing in the darkness of their closet, gun pointed at the door, and tears running down her face.

Chapter 15

The dispatcher's voice interjected, "Ma'am, the police have arrived. They informed me that they are walking around the perimeter of the house. You are going to be alright."

The sounds of sirens were present in the background. Cammie began to feel relieved. As she lowered the gun, the door opened and light flooded her eyes.

She screamed and the deafening sound of a gun going off pierced the ears of everyone on the phone.

Seth and the operator waited for the next sound. Their ears were ringing. Cammie was making an attempt to catch her breath.

The first words they heard come over the phone was, "Police! Police! Put your weapon down on the floor. Put down the gun and slowly come out of the closet. You are safe now, put down the gun!"

Seth waited, he feared that his wife might have shot an officer. He prayed that he would not hear 'Officer Down, Officer Down.'

"Ma'am, it is alright. You are safe. Please put down the gun."

Seth could picture his wife in shock, not able to will her body to put down the weapon.

"Honey, dear, you need to put down the gun. The police are there and you are going to be fine. You did good. I'm proud of you. You did it! You saved yourself and the kids. You did good. Now put down the gun."

Seth could hear the gun make connection with the wood flooring. Next he heard his kids crying. He wished more than anything that he could be there with them.

"CAMMIE, DON'T LET THE KIDS SEE HIM! DON'T LET THEM SEE! COVER THEIR EYES! DO YOU HEAR ME?"

Chapter 16

Tessy threw the phone back in her purse and ran with the other shoppers toward the commotion. It wasn't every day that something exciting happened at the grocery store and the fact that Jack was not answering his phone caused her great distress.

She quickly had images of Jack arguing with another customer over a piece of steak. What was wrong with her man? What was this new obsession with meat? She just hoped that he hadn't gotten into a fistfight over a T-bone.

As she turned the corner her eyes widened as she slid to a stop on the slick flooring. Everyone was in awe. It appeared that nobody knew what to do. Tessy stood there with eyes and mouth wide open, staring at the man she thought she knew well.

Jack was face first and up to his waist in the butcher display case. Meat had fallen all over the floor. Blood was running down Jack's arms and legs and spreading across the floor. Jack was clawing at the packages with his fingers and teeth like a ravaged beast. Nobody dared approach him. The crowd continued to grow. Tessy knew that soon the local police would show up and escort her husband out in handcuffs.

Chapter 17

Scott was a retired police officer who took a job as a security
guard at the local grocery store for some extra cash. The job
mostly consisted of greeting customers, chatting with friends, and
occasionally chasing shoplifting kids. In all his years on the force,
he had never seen this before.

The lone security guard cautiously approached the man that was
waste deep into a stack of meat in the butcher's department.
From a distance, the guard called out to him. Oblivious to his
surroundings, the man continued to feast. The guard pulled out
his club and nudged the man's hip. Absentmindedly, he brushed
the stick away as if it were a pesky fly. The security guard looked
helpless. He looked around the crowd as if soliciting ideas.
Slowly a woman in her thirties, maybe early forties, nicely dressed
and pretty but apparently in shock approached him.

The security guard recognized the woman's face. She and her
husband shopped there every Sunday evening together. The
thought brought him the realization. He asked if the man was her
husband and she nodded nervously. He cautioned her closer and
invited her to do something.

Chapter 18

Tessy was frightened. Jack had done some strange things in life, often playing pranks or acting out for the shock effect. But this was beyond anything he had done, this was strange, this was scary. She called out to him, but he seemed to not hear her. She struggled to get his name out with more volume; nothing but grunts and snorts. She found herself beginning to cry and despised her weakness.

Finally she mustered up her strength and with utter frustration yelled,
"JAAAACCCKKKKK!!!!"

The grunting and snorting stopped. Jack brought up his head, wiped his face on his sleeve and looked around. He seemed shocked, as if waking from a dream. He looked down at his arms, body, and legs. He seemed to gain consciousness of his surroundings and what he had been doing.

He looked back at the meat, at the mess on the floor, at himself, and then at the crowd, finally his eyes found Tessy. His face melted into a form of a little boy asking for help. Tessy's heart ached. She approached him, but did not want to touch him. She gingerly grabbed the back of one arm and coaxed him through the crowd and out the doors. She expected someone to stop them, expecting charges for the damages, an arrest to be made, something. But nobody said anything, they just watched as the couple slowly exited the store. The only sound being the music playing on the store's intercom system.

Chapter 19

Paul and Dillon entered the bar together. It was obvious what they were up to; dressed in all black, including a night man's cap. Their apparel really didn't matter; they were among friends.

This was a local's bar, made up of men from the Parks neighborhood. Most of the patrons were on the same page, forming their own patrols. The only difference was that the boys had dressed like they were snipers. To somebody who did not know what was going on, they might suspect them of robbing vacant homes.

Curtis, one of the old timers, took the opportunity to deliver a ribbing.

"You 'soldiers' be careful out there fighting the war. Keep things safe for the rest of us, alright?"

Curtis had to be one of the oldest guys in the Parks subdivision, definitely the oldest regular at Raliegh's. He served in one of the old wars, but nobody could get a straight answer out of him. Most the time he was too drunk to understand, but when he was sober, he enjoyed teasing so much that one could never tell if his stories were true. At various times Curtis had shared stories that included him fighting in Vietnam, Korea, and both WWI & II.

Nick had asked him if he also had fought in the Gulf War, this truly upset Curtis. His response was that he maybe old, but he was still young enough to kick Nick's butt and teach him a lesson in respecting his elders.

Paul and Dillon grabbed their Pabst Blue Ribbons from Sahara, said a quick hello, and found a vacant table to wait for the others.

"NICK," Dillon called out as soon as Nicholas had entered the bar.

Nick popped his head to acknowledge that he saw them, and then made his way to the bar.

As Nick was chatting with Sahara, Gregory bounced into the bar. He shook a few hands and made his traditional rounds. He always said hello to everyone before making it to the bar to order a drink. Paul believed he did this to try and score free drinks – it usually worked.

Nick and Gregory eventually made it over to the table where the rest of the boys sat.

"You girls done socializing or are you hoping to be asked to dance," Paul chastised.

Nick lowered his gaze, and then he took a swig from his bottle.

Gregory gave Paul a crooked smile, exposing his white teeth, perfectly aligned from the veneers he was forced to have installed. His mother believed that all water was polluted and resolved that Coke was safer. So Gregory was raised on Coke. Even as a baby, his mother gave him Coke in a bottle. His teeth didn't stand a chance, and around the age of 17, his dentist suggested veneers.

"Ok, enough with wasting time. Let's down these beers, do a shot of Jagermeister, and head out," Paul ordered.

Chapter 20

Every year, Malcolm enjoyed heading to the Sierras to camp and backpack. He loved to hike, loved the outdoors, and loved the solitude. His annual tradition occurred each year, just before hunting season opened up. He loved this time of year because it afforded him the opportunity to see the most wildlife.

He began backpacking alone, in his early twenties, when a group of guys all bailed out on a trip. He was determined to go, with or without them. So he loaded up his gear and had the most rewarding trip of his existence.

Hiking alone, he was able to travel faster and more quietly. Most animals were busy grazing or sleeping, unaware that Malcolm was hunting them with his Nikon SLR. He had more pictures of wild life than he could ever figure out what to do with.

He shook his head every time a person would complain that they never saw any animals on their trips to the mountains. He would pass others on the trails; hear them from about a mile away, talking, singing, and gear clinking with every step. If he could hear them with his inferior human hearing from a mile, the animals could easily hear them from several miles away.

He worried about de-evolution of mankind. If society ever collapsed and people could not obtain substance at their local supermarkets… holes could not be dug fast enough to bury all of the bodies. Though most of modern society was only a couple of generations removed from agriculture, the skills were long forgotten. Most people had not a clue how to farm, hunt, kill, or prepare a kill. Civilized societies would turn into gangs of scavengers.

Malcolm had hiked for two days, deep into the High Sierras. He started off at the Crabtree trailhead and headed east on the dusty trail. He quickly passed by the crowded attraction of Grouse Lake. It was difficult to find a camp spot here and he wondered why anyone would want to spend the night there. The mosquito population was unbearable.

Malcolm swatted the flies and mosquitos with his wide-brimmed hat, a hat that began as a dark chocolate colored felt. Now after years of abuse and miles of protecting his head and neck from the scorching Sierra sun, it had faded into a tannish-green.

With his mouth closed and head down, Malcolm powered through what he referred to as the Mosquito filter. Here, most people became so irritated by the curtain of bugs, that they turned and high-tailed it back to the city. Malcolm welcomed the bugs; it meant that there would be less people in the high country.

After traveling through the short mile of constant buzzing, he began his ascent up the large granite boulders and deeper into the wild. With the combination of large steps and thin high altitude air, many people struggled with the climb. Like the mosquito filter, Malcolm met the tough climb with affection.

He dragged his palm along the smooth granite. Millions of years of slow moving glaciers had polished and carved the cliffs that he now hiked along. He absorbed energy from the rock and continued his journey.

Occasionally, a small trickle of water or a spring would appear along the trail. Here he would fill up his hiking hat and quickly place it over his head. The freezing snowmelt was invigorating and instantly cooled off heated skin. Never had he tasted more delicious water than that water that traveled through the granite rocks of the Sierras.

Malcolm was careful to treat the water he drank up here. From the thousands of visitors each year, and the mixed-use of cattle grazing, the pure waters were teaming with Giardia Intestinalis. This bacterium made grown men cry. The abdomen cramps could immobilize a hiker. The diarrhea and resulting dehydration could kill a person in a number of days.

A person who was only out for an overnighter could seek immediate medical attention with the onset of symptoms and increase his/her chance of survival.

But a person who was in the woods for a week or so, like Malcolm, the symptoms could overcome them and prevent them from returning or seeking medical assistance. The chances of death increased exponentially when hiking alone. Nobody was there to fetch help.

So Malcolm always treated his drinking water with iodine tablets or by boiling the water with his Jet Boil. He hated to do so because it took away much of the taste from the rock and minerals that he loved. To make up for it, he allowed himself the guilty pleasure of suckling on a fresh trickle of water that had an obvious source straight from the rock.

It was impossible to drink nature's refreshment without finishing the indulgence with an exhalation of air, signifying the level of satisfaction received. The cold liquid could be felt as it traveled through his mouth, past his tonsils, down his throat, contracting his windpipe, and chilling his esophagus before gathering in his stomach.

Malcolm filled up his hat once again, placed it on his head, and turned his gaze skyward as a red-tailed hawk screeched overhead. The bird kited on the thermals that rose from the heated granite. The bird's head jerked back and forth as he scanned the forest below him, presumably searching for the next meal.

Malcolm stood up, propped his 35-pound backpack on his bent knee, and swung the bag around to his backside while simultaneously threading his arms into the arm straps. He hopped once and pulled his waist straps tight, distributing the weight of his load to carry evenly on his hips. Then he placed his sunglasses back on his face and continued on his trek.

Chapter 21

Cammie could not bring herself to talk, but she did hear her husband screaming into her earpiece. She knew that she was not finished protecting her children from this intruder. She listened to her husband and her body switched to autopilot. She was shaking and having trouble breathing. Without much thought, her body instinctually beckoned her children. She was able to gather her little boy and girl and bury their faces into her abdomen like a hen gathering her chicks.

She could not pull her eyes away from the man that lay sprawled on the floor in front of her. A man who had came so close to hurting her and her babies. She stared at the body of the man, sprawled open, skin pulled back from the gunshot wound that she had delivered. A puddle of blood was slowly growing around the torso of the man.

Her gaze travelled up the torso, the blood stained neck, and finally on the face that was splattered with blood. She looked at the man, a white male in his early forties, greasy brown hair, and a five-day beard. She had no idea who this person was or why he wanted them so much.

An officer slowly and carefully stepped over the man, interrupting the trance that had Cammie frozen in place. She watched as the man gingerly reached for the shotgun that laid at her feet. He pulled at it, and then slowly handed it back through the doorway to another uniformed man.

She had never seen the gun before. She knew that her husband had several guns, but never saw this one. Never even saw him clean it, when he ritually cleaned all of his guns. The shotgun was short, as far as shotguns were concerned.

Why did Seth have a sawed-off shotgun, she wondered?

As if answering her own question, an officer corrected another cop by explaining that it was not sawn-off, but was a shotgun built short and meant for home defense.

She watched as the guy emptied the four remaining shells onto the floor.

"Gun is emptied and secured," he announced.

Another man spread a sheet over the man lying on the floor. Then the officer nearest to Cammie began speaking calmly and quietly. Cammie had problems hearing what he was saying to her. She tried to concentrate on his face and the words that he spoke.

"Ma'am? Ma'am? Can you hear me? Everything is ok now. You are going to be all right. I'm going to get you and your kids out of here now. Let me have your children. Ma'am? Ma'am, you need to let go now. Come on. We are here to help."

Cammie wanted to cooperate. She willed her body to respond, but she could not get her arms to let go of her kids. She felt the man gently prying her arm away from her boy. She willed to comply, but her arm remained rigid. She could not shake out of the fog that engulfed her head.

The officer gently removed her small boy from her grasp and carefully handed him over the dead body to another officer. Cammie watched the procedure from within the confines of the mummy that had once been her body. The officer then performed the exact same maneuver with her sobbing girl.

Though her children were merely five feet from her, she hated being apart. She longed to have them back in her arms. Her motherly instincts were in overdrive, but her mind was still in a crippling fog.

The officer gently grabbed her left arm with both of his hands. He escorted her out of the closet and directed her steps so as to not disturb the dead heap on her bedroom floor.

The other officer took her by the right arm and walked her over to her waiting children. Instantly, the three of them collided in a mass of bodies, embracing arms, and sounds of whimpering.

The officers slowly coaxed the family out of the bedroom and down to the living room.

Chapter 22

Awaking with the rising sun and the call of the birds around his tent, Malcolm stretched and then quickly hobbled out of his sleeping bag and tent. He did not bother with shoes on his feet. The first and only thing on his mind was to relieve himself of the urine that had built up all night and was threatening to breach the damn at any moment.

He danced around as he struggled to navigate the pine comb covered ground to the tree nearest to his tent. He was poised to begin the release of fluid moments before he had reached the destination. His body shivered as the cold morning breeze crossed Cherry Creek and greeted his exposed genitals. Malcolm shook his body to ward off the goose bumps forming on his legs and arms.

Returning to his camp, he now found the time to slide his dirty bare feet into his boots. He poured water from his Nalgene into the Jet Boil and fired up the flame.

The Jet Boil roared to life and his mouth began to water with anticipation of breakfast: instant oatmeal and coffee. His stomach growled as if to confirm that it was indeed empty.

After consuming three packets of instant oatmeal, Malcolm fetched his fishing rod, bait, and squishy mug of coffee and headed down to the Creek. After washing the sticky pinesap from the souls of his feet, he found a somewhat flat boulder next to the creek and perched himself on top. He cast his baited line into an eddy, his line finding perfect purchase on the boulder creating the calm pool.

Malcolm settled into the granite seat and reached for his mug of Joe, mindful not to squeeze the soft-sided mug. He had mindlessly grabbed his mug on numerous occasions, resulting in the hot beverage breaching the container and scalding his fist. Even so, he still found the benefit of a lightweight collapsible silicone mug far outweighed the risk of a burnt hand.

He slowly sipped the warm goodness, savoring the taste as he held the liquid in his mouth before sending it down his throat and into his belly. He sat there on his pew, waiting for a fish to approach his bait.

He paid more attention to his surroundings than he did to his line. These forests were his sanctuary. He came here, not only to escape the hustle and bustle of city life, but also to commune with his maker.

His maker welcomed him to this place of worship with soothing sounds of birds chirping and water flowing over rocks. The brisk morning air made him feel alive. The down puffy jacket provided the warmth and soft comfort of a mother's embrace.

Malcolm never expected to catch any fish on his outings. In the many years that he had been venturing on these expeditions, he had only caught one Rainbow trout. He knew that hiking in early fall reduced his chances of catching anything in the streams and lakes that had been overfished by summer visitors. He fished anyway because of the calming experience.

After finishing his coffee, Malcolm sat and meditated for another 10 minutes before rinsing his mug and pulling in the line. He headed back to camp.

Within 7 minutes, Malcolm had his camp broken down and backpack loaded. He raised his hands to heaven and arched his back as he stretched up onto his toes. His body was feeling the long hike of the day before and the night of sleeping on the ground.

He performed a few more stretching techniques before securing his gear on his back. With full water containers and belly, he set out on his trek to go deeper into the woods and further away from civilization.

Somewhere Southeast of Wood Lake, Malcolm took off up a slab of rock that took him off trail, heading northeast. He had been here once before, once when he had gotten lost.

Years prior, Malcolm was crossing the barren exposed granite slab. The only way of navigating these slabs was to follow the cairn markers, erected by hikers and park rangers. Cairn markers consisted of stacking rocks, usually three high. A cairn is obviously manmade and oddly sticks out in the wilderness. Purest often kicked over the trail markers, offended by the obvious signs of previous human visitors. Malcolm wondered about the irony of how the Cairns was so offensive while, the trail they travelled on somehow was not.

He figured that the Cairns had been dismantled and thus the reason for him losing his way. With only a map and compass, he navigated over ridges and down cliffs, to a nearby trail illustrated on his map.

The trail turned out to be more of a game trail and intermittent at that. Upon checking out at the US Forest Station, Malcolm discovered that his map was outdated and that the trail had been abandoned several decades prior. It was not illustrated on modern maps.

Malcolm was off trail, off the grid, and lost for 28 hours. He successfully self-rescued, scaling over a long sloping granite mountain and serendipitously discovering a well-travelled trail.

Consequently, the bonus of going off trail, he discovered, was a large High Sierra valley, absent of intrusive trails. Without readily available accessibility, this section of forest was essentially untouched by humans.

Since that trip, Malcolm had wanted to return to this valley. He knew that his next visit would be much more enjoyable without the heavy cloud of anxiety over being lost and vulnerable, miles from anybody.

In preparation, he spent hours examining the area on his topographic maps. He studied the area on Google Earth. He highlighted his own trail to be blazed, based on what he presumed would be the easiest entry and exit points. He also highlighted three alternative possibilities. And as an added precaution, this time he left explicit details with his wife, just encase something should go wrong.

Chapter 23

Brenda dreaded every autumn when her husband would take off to the woods. She did not understand his insistent attitude to backpack alone. She worried for months leading up to his annual outings. While he was gone, she would constantly watch the news and search the Internet for word of lost or injured hikers. She obsessed over weather reports.

Anytime she came upon a report of bear attacks or lost hikers needing rescue, she would email them or hang them in his office. He understood her concerns, but recharging his batteries in Nature was simply how he prevented himself from going crazy.

For years, his practice involved taking to the woods without leaving a trace behind him. He relished in knowing that nobody knew where he was and nobody would be able to find him. It was just he, the wild, and his maker.

After falling in love with Brenda, he became more responsible and sensitive to her worries. He now left her with specific plans for his mecca. A copy of the map, highlighted route, list of stops, contact information for the Ranger stations, and expected date of return. Despite the added weight, he also carried the Spot that she had given him for Christmas.

The Spot was a device that tracked his whereabouts. Brenda could log onto the website and find out where Malcolm had last checked in. Malcolm periodically pulled out the spot device and pushed the appropriate button: 'I'm O.K.' or 'Help, come and get me – release the hounds.' If the latter were selected, a call to the local Ranger and Search and Rescue would be made. His GPS coordinates would be relayed and -assuming he stayed put – they could find and assist him.

Brenda also insisted that he carry a GPS unit to help prevent him from getting lost. Malcolm hated carrying anything that required batteries, but he conceded to appease his wife.

She had hoped that the devices that he agreed to carry would help subside her anxiety, but it did very little except cause her to routinely log on to see if he needed help.

Malcolm begged his wife to take her own vacation to get away and free her mind of worry. But she resisted. She could not bear being away, should Malcolm require her assistance.

She had thought of threatening to leave him in attempts to motivate him to cease his dangerous pastime, but she refrained out of fear that he just might call her bluff. She avoided the devastation of finding out that her husband would choose the mountains over her. Instead she resorted to complaining, whining, nagging, and begging each year as he prepared for his retreat.

Malcolm was a good man and a terrific husband. He never looked at other women, had no interest in pornography, refrained from gambling, and never wasted a weekend with watching football. Brenda knew she was fortunate to have him as a husband, but it did not ease her mind while he was gone.

Each night, the couple would stare up at the sky. Locating Orion, their eyes would focus on the middle star that made up the constellation's belt. They had agreed to do this any night that they were apart. Knowing that the other was gazing at the same star at the same moment had an overwhelming blanket of emotion that connected the couple despite the miles of separation.

Brenda fell asleep on the back deck, wrapped up in the family quilt that Malcolm's Grandmother had made.

She awoke with a startle. Her subconscious had registered a foreign sound in the yard. She lay frozen in place, straining to find the source of the noise that had interrupted her dreams.

She could see her breath, hear her heartbeat, and attempted to suppress the sound of her breathing. The music played softly inside the house. She had the radio tuned to KOIT 96.5, listening to the program *Love Songs After Dark.* The moon had cast a bright eerie blue shade across the backyard.

Brenda tried to scan her surroundings without moving her head. Her eyes moved in their sockets, ears trained on the sounds of night. Without hearing additional movement, Brenda cautiously rose off the lounge chair and stood up on the firm redwood deck boards. With her back to the house and her eyes trained on the yard, she slowly backed toward the slider.

Blindly reaching behind her back, she slowly slid the screen, wheels following the track. She never realized how loud the screen sounded. She took one step backward into the house when she heard a noise coming from within the house.

She froze, one leg in the house the other trying to decide on which side of the threshold to be placed. Brenda forced herself to turn around and investigate the source of the sound.

As she turned around, she contemplated on how similar the sound was to someone eating. She could make out the distinguished sound of saliva rich chewing.

Willing herself toward the kitchen, she took slow quiet steps toward the sound. For the first time ever, she felt that she was more at risk at home than her husband was out in the woods.

She inched herself toward the kitchen. She peered over the peninsula, trying to gain a vantage point while keeping something solid between them.

She could hear the chomping, the slurping, and the swallowing. She just could not see what was going on. She quietly and carefully climbed onto a barstool. Propping herself with her arms on the bar, she raised herself higher and leaned over the cabinetry.

"AAAAAAAAAAAAAGGHHHH," she couldn't help screaming when she saw the large hunk of fur digging in her garbage.

When the face turned and looked at her with glowing eyes, long bitty nose, and haggled teeth, she lost her footing. She slammed down on the bar and bounced off onto the floor.

The possum ran right past her feet and out the screen door. The creepy hairless tale left a trail of spaghetti sauce along her floor.

Brenda's heartbeat felt like it would thump through her chest. She struggled to regain her breath. The possum was so ugly and scary looking. She hated the things.

How did it get into the house, she wondered.

Brenda got back on her feet and walked over to close the screen door. She pulled the door close, and then she noticed that the screen material was loose along the bottom corner. She bent down and upon investigation determined that the possum had sneaked through the screen as she slept on the deck.

As she closed the slider, she took one more look at the night sky. She gazed at Orion's belt wondering if her husband was awake and doing the same.

She let out a silent prayer, "*God, please protect my love. Please watch over him. Allow him to return home safe and unscathed. I have been so blessed to have him in my life. Please continue to shower me with your grace. Amen and Goodnight.*"

With that, Brenda finished closing the door and locked it.

Chapter 24

As soon as Tessy got Jack back into the house, she began
speaking to him as if nothing out of the ordinary had happened.
She treated him as if he had a bad day, nothing more. She knew
that Jack wished not to discuss the incident at the grocery store;
besides, she had no idea what she would say.

"I'm going to draw you a bath and pour you some wine, ok
Honey?" She yelled from the hallway.

Jack could hear the water turn on and begin splashing into the
bottom of the tub. He visualized the large tub and the splashing of
the water as it hit the base of the tub.

He remodeled the master bathroom a few years back. They had
turned the master bedroom and bath into a nice spa-like retreat.
The tub he installed was 6 feet long and four feet deep. It was
deep enough and long enough for the two of them to enjoy a
relaxing soak. The 8-foot picture window sat down flush with the
tub deck surround and gave a direct view of their master bedroom
patio area.

This also had a spa-like feel, with a couple of pillowed chairs framing an outdoor fire pit. The far side of the patio had a natural screen made of flowering Morning Glories and Jasmine. Ever since the remodel, the couple spent a majority of their time at home back on the patio.

Tessy treated every bad day or foul mood with a soak in the bath. Jack did not see how a bath was going to improve this situation.

Jack stood in the foyer of their small track home. He closed the front door and then stood there, unable to make any sense of the day's events. He listened as his wife got his bath ready and uncorked a bottle of wine. He looked down at his shirt; it was wet and cold with blood. The shirt clung to his chest and stomach.

His wife appeared with two towels. She spread out one in front of him on the floor and coaxed him to step forward. She then helped him remove his stained clothes. These clothes were beyond recovery. She had him place them into a garbage bag.

Jack stood naked before his wife; cold, wet, and shivering. He began to cry.

Tessy had never seen Jack cry before. The closest she ever witnessed was when his dog died. Even then, Jack merely choked up as he said his goodbyes. It broke Tessy's heart to hear the quiver in his voice. She wondered what went on in a man's mind when he forcibly held back emotions. But here he stood before her, a broken man. She gently dried his skin and offered soft soothing words of comfort. She hid the tears that began streaking down her face.

Chapter 25

Jack and Tessy had been married just 5 years, but since the moment they first laid eyes on each other, they felt that they had known each other their whole existence.

When they first met, they both instantly knew that they were meant to be together. Both of them had been through numerous relationships, never quite satisfied for one reason or another. Then they finally found each other.

They had a short courtship, and in the absence of any doubt, they quickly married and never looked back. They absolutely loved each other. To watch them behave with each other was like watching a couple that had been married for 50 years. They knew each other inside and out.

And so it pained Tessy to see Jack like this. For the first time, she wondered if she really knew the man she shared her life with. She feared him slipping mentally. As she led him down the main hallway, back toward the bath she had drawn him, she had a premonition of what old age might be like. She shivered at the thought that she may need to begin caring for him far too soon.

She quickly chased the thought from her mind.

"Jack, I have your bath drawn just how you like it; luke warm – not too hot. I have a bottle of your favorite wine, Sauvignon Blanc from our trip to Wilson Vineyard, and two glasses for us to share."

Jack could not respond. He heard his wife and truly appreciated her efforts. He knew she was trying to understand and be supportive. But how could she ever understand, he did not even understand. He wondered if he was really losing his marbles.

Tessy helped Jack lower his body into the tub. He settled in as she poured the wine into the two glasses. Jack wondered now, as he often did, how he ever was lucky enough to find Tessy and convince her to spend her life with him. He never felt that he deserved her, but relished in every moment they spent together.

Jack took the glass of wine that his wife offered him; he held the glass to his nose and inhaled the aromas that lifted off the liquid in the glass. His mind drifted and considered the resemblance of blood in the fine wine. He thought about how the wine paired nicely with barbequed tri-tip. He shook his head and scrunched his brow.

"What's wrong," Tessy inquired.

"Nothing honey, I just am so sorry. I do not deserve you."

Tessy's heart ached for her lover. She smoothed his hair back with a wet hand and kissed his forehead.

"True, you do not deserve me, so don't screw it up by telling me."

She smiled and Jack made an attempt.

"Here, I know what this moment is missing."

Tessy stood up from her chair and flipped the switch on the wall. Instantly the gas fireplace at the end of the tub sprung to life. The fireplace was Jack's idea. A double-sided fireplace could be seen from the tub on one side and from their bed on the other side.

Jack lost his gaze in the dancing of the flames. Fire always mesmerized him. He loved sitting next to a campfire and watching the fire breath and dance as it consumed the logs.

Tessy was comforted by the content look on Jack's face as he gazed into the fire. She came to the conclusion that come what might, things would be ok. She and Jack would stand together and work through things.

Chapter 26

Seth Parker rushed home. He was extremely worried about his wife and kids. He could not wrap his head around what had happened.

They lived in a safe neighborhood. So it was extremely unusual and troubling that an intruder had entered their house. It was the mid-morning, and this sort of thing just did not happen here.

Seth knew he was risking a ticket, but he could not get home to his loved ones fast enough. He raced up Highway 680, flew through the High Speed Fastrak toll-lane of Benicia Bridge, and was home in less than half the normal time.

He double-parked in front of his house, blocking in several squad cars. He jumped out of his still running vehicle and ran toward the house.

A uniformed officer intercepted Seth before he even reached his driveway.

Before he could tell the guy who he was; the neighborhood yelled in unison that he lived there.

The officer let him pass and Seth sprinted through the front door.

"CAMMIE?" Seth bellowed in the foyer.

"Right here, honey. We're right here."

The two children left the arms of their mother and ran to Seth, jumping into his arms. Seth picked both kids up and hobbled to his wife.

Cammie stood up from the leather sofa and embraced her family. She began sobbing uncontrollably.

She had held herself together for the sake of her kids, but at the site of her husband, Cammie allowed her emotions the release they were begging for. Seth wept and kissed his wife and two kids repeatedly.

The officers in the room walked into the hall and then outside to allow the family a personal moment.

Against the protest of his children, Seth placed them on the couch. He then grasped his wife's face with both his hands. He placed a kiss on her forehead and one on her quivering lip. Then he looked into her tear-filled eyes.

"Honey, you did so good. You saved our family. I am eternally grateful for what you did. I am so proud of you. I'm sorry that I was not here for you, I'm so so sorry," Seth said soothingly.

He brushed her wet hair away from her cheeks.

She replied, "No, no babe, you were here for us. I could not have done that without your help. I was a wreck and you kept me together. Like everything else, we did it together."

The couple embraced and the children jumped up and wrapped their arms around their legs.

Chapter 27

The police walked back in and cleared their throats to announce
their presence. Seth and Cammie broke their embrace and gave
the men their attention. The each lifted up a child into their arms.

"I'm sorry, I know that this is terribly... hard on your family, I'm
truly sorry. I don't have to tell you that our town just never sees
this kind of thing. Oakland, Richmond, sure, but not here."

Seth and Cammie nodded their heads in agreement. The officer
continued.

"I know that this will be difficult, but we'd like to remove the guy
from your house, but before we do, we really need to see if you
can identify the guy. This would help us piece together what
happened here."

Seth nodded his head and handed his son to his wife.

"You guys stay here, you've been through enough."

Seth walked with the officer to the master bedroom.

As he approached the room, he saw a sea of uniforms, flashing bulbs from cameras, and heard several conversations occurring simultaneously.

The officer belted out, "Make some room!"

The room instantly went silent and the body of men parted like the Red Sea.

The officer bent down at the body, grabbed the sheet, and glanced up at Seth. Seth looked down at him, took a deep breath, and then nodded his head.

The officer slowly pulled back the sheet exposing the blood stained face of the man that had broken into his home and terrorized Seth's family.

Seth fought the urge to stomp on the dead man's head. He knew what the officer wanted, but he had a difficult time seeing through the rage. All he could see was red. He forced himself to gain his composure and his vision cleared.

He concentrated on the man's face; he tried to imagine what the man looked like absent the blood. Finally the realization of who the man was hit him like a Mack truck.

The officer saw the recognition on Seth's face.

"You know this man, who is it? Seth, who is this? Mr. Parker, tell us who this man is!"

Seth sounded confused, "he's our next door neighbor. I-I-I don't understand. Why would he do this?"

Chapter 28

Paul was the ringleader. Whenever the guys decided to do anything beyond hanging out at Raliegh's, it was always Paul who took over the reigns.

The boys finished their drinks and headed out of the pub and into the night.

They all jumped into Paul's Mitsubishi Lancer and made their way out of the parking lot. Just as Paul was selecting drive, they saw Kyle walking across the parking lot.

Kyle was a 17-year-old kid from the Parks Subdivision. He was a good kid and mature for his age. Many people mistakenly thought he was 21, which made obtaining beers easier for him. He walked up to the car when he heard the guys calling out to him.

"What's going on guys? Woe, what's up with the garbs?"

"Nothing, we're just going to try and catch the dude who's taking everyone's pets," Paul told him.

"Really!? Mars went missing a week ago. Nobody can find him. No broken fence boards, gate was closed, no holes, nothing. Oh, and get this, his leash is missing," Kyle informed.

"Cops are claiming there's a mountain lion that came down out of the foothills. I don't buy it. Mountain lions don't use leashes when they take animals," Kyle stated.

"Eh, kid, sorry about your dog, somebody took mine as well," Nick consoled.

"Yeah, well I'd like to know who's doing this, I'd slit his throat or beat his head in," Kyle told the boys.

"Hey, jump in, come with us. Maybe we'll get lucky tonight and find the guy," Paul offered.

"Yea? Really? Ok."

Kyle joined the guys in the back seat and the car lurched forward toward the street.

Chapter 29

The car came to a stop along the curb just outside of Rix Park.

Rix Park was the neighborhood park that was more of a green belt. When the neighborhood was first constructed, the park stretched 4 miles. It was the quickest way to get from one end of the development to the other. It connected a pre-school, elementary school, and several playgrounds. It also connected to a flood canal at one point. The flood canal stretched for miles and miles around the city.

The boys decided to begin their patrol by clearing Rix Park. They set off on foot, with Dillon humming the theme song to Mission Impossible. The other guys got into it and they began sneaking between trees, bushes, and rolling on the ground.

They carried an assortment of weapons in their arsenal; a bat, a golf club, and various knives. Unbeknownst to the rest of the gang, Dillon carried his new 45 Magnum, hidden beneath his waistband in the small of his back. He had the weapon as an insurance policy; none of the guys truly knew what they might encounter.

Within half-a-mile, the boys fell into formation; walking shoulder-to-shoulder and doing more talking than searching. The mission had lost the clandestine aspect and the boys resorted to talk of sports, girls, and life.

Within an hour, they had covered just over half of the greenbelt. Each time they came to a residential road crossing, they briefly revisited the practice of stealth mode. Anyone watching would easily see the 5 guys darting across the street, their covertness thwarted by the strategically placed streetlights.

The mission continually turned into jovial pranks at the road crossings. The boys tripped and pushed each other. They pulled caps and shirts over each other's heads. Paul gave Dillon a Charlie-Horse right as he stepped into the light. This made Dillon squeal and prevented a hasty crossing. Everyone giggled, except for Dillon – who would have laughed had it been anybody else.

Dillon obtained revenge on Paul by de-pancing him at the next crossing. All of the boys lost composure upon learning that he wasn't wearing underpants. They lost self-control and laughed out loud, some showboating by rolling on the grass as Paul struggled to get his pants back up. He hobbled over to the shadows and collapsed onto the grass, his pants tripping him up.

The boys continued to laugh until a nearby house flipped on a security light that illuminated the portion of the park where they resided. The boys quickly gained their composure and ran deeper into the park.

"Hey Paulie, how come you are not wearing underwear? Did you have to ditch them after crapping your pants," Nick ribbed.

Everyone else began laughing again.

"Shut up Nicker. We're on a mission, so I'm sporting commando style."

"Well, GI Joe, try and keep it in your pants next time; nobody's interested."

"Ha, ha, if you weren't so interested, why did you stare for so long," Paul retorted while pulsating his eyebrows and making kissing sounds.

"Well between the moles and the forest you got growing down there, I couldn't help but stare at your train wreck."

Lacking a response, Paul slugged Nick's upper arm while tripping him. Again everyone laughed.

Chapter 30

The guys approached another road crossing. Everglades was one of the major arteries to the Parks subdivision. Though the road was still only single-lane, it was considerably wider to allow for buses and emergency vehicles.

The flood canal –referred to in the neighborhood as "The Creek"- dove under the road at the same crossing. The elementary school backed up to the creek, sharing a chain-linked fence. Many of the kids made use of the "shortcut" to get to and from school. They would crawl under the chain-link fence that separated the creek from Rix Park, carefully navigate across the creek via strategically placed rocks, scramble up the dirt embankment, and hop over the school fence after tossing over a book bag.

The short cut only shaved a mere 3 minutes – unless running to avoid detection was employed. The Principal threatened detention for anyone caught climbing fences. In reality, nobody ever received much more than a scolding from the morning yard-duty.

The five boys approached the Everglades crossing with caution.

The crossing was the busiest of all the Rix Park crossings. If they were to be spotted or caught, this was the most likely of all places.

Their pace slowed and they crept along, protected in the shadows of the unlit park. No headlights were visible on the road and so far they could not see anybody out for a late night stroll. The gang moved forward in sync, approaching the road.

"Ok, no foolin around this time, agreed?" Paul ordered.

Nobody verbalized the compliance, but everyone agreed.

The guys swept their surroundings as they advanced. Nick was center, flanked on the left by Dillon and Gregory and on the right by Paul and Kyle.

Dillon and Gregory scanned the Creek and schoolyard, hoping to see movement of the guy they were searching for. Nick had his eyes on the park that continued on the other side of the road. Paul scanned the road in anticipation of a passing vehicle. Kyle scanned the right side of the park.

"Coast is clear, let's move," Paul ordered.

The group began to hustle, nearing the edge where the shadows turned to light from the illumination cast from the streetlight. Just as they began to hasten their forward motion, an annoyingly bright overhead light lighted up their surroundings. It was not until this moment that the boys recognized the sound of a helicopter high over head.

Without even looking up, all five boys scattered. Dillon and Gregory took off to the left, running up Everglades and then a right onto Yellowstone. Nick, Paul, and Kyle made a break to the right up Everglades.

Chapter 31

The Sheriff's office was a buzz with people running everywhere and shouting. Sheriff Glasgow had been receiving countless reports of missing pets. Tonight he performed a public announcement on the evening news suggesting that people keep their pets inside. He attempted to guise the warning under the presumption of a wandering mountain lion. He did not expect anyone to buy into that explanation. Typically a mountain lion would repeatedly hit a particular neighborhood until it was caught. These incidents were happening all over the county.

Now, as the Sheriff stood in his office looking out, he could see that his service announcement only caused a commotion. His office was filled with people wanting to report their missing pets. He wondered how long it would be before vigilante groups formed and began roaming the streets.

"Sheriff, the Medical Examiner is here" Deputy Blayne Stevens interrupted his thought process.

"Ok, great, send her in" the Sheriff responded.

"Hello Sheriff," Blythe Aspen stated as she offered him her hand.

"Thank you for coming right over on short notice," the Sheriff responded.

"No problem, it looks like things have really hit the fan here," Blythe offered.

Blythe Aspen was an intelligent and attractive woman in her early thirties. She always dressed professional. While most in her field sported the typical hospital scrubs all day long, she insisted on looking her best outside of the labs. Today was no exception. She looked ravishing in a black dress, accented by white trim. The dress was classy and modest, though the form-fitting outfit could not hide her curves. On her feet she wore standard pumps that were shined to a mirror finish. Rather than reporting for duty, she looked like she would be heading out for cocktails.

She never carried a purse or sports bag. Instead, she maintained her professional persona with a business-only looking briefcase. When she opened the case, one might suspect her profession to be a torturer. Undoubtedly, the first things to catch a person's eye were the shiny stainless steel surgeon tools. Each in their appropriate place, strapped behind bungee webbing stitched into the lid of the briefcase. Next, the eyes would trace down to the surgeon gown, neatly folded over and hiding the rest of her personal affects.

The Sheriff respected her opinion. As soon as his animal control unit began bringing in the devoured animal carcasses, he knew he wanted to talk to Blythe Aspen.

"Ms. Aspen, I do not wish to waste any of your time, so I will cut straight to the point. My animal control units have been bringing in devoured animal corpses. I'm sure that you have heard that pets have been going missing? What I'd like for you to do is take a look at these remains and see if you can tell what is eating them," the Sheriff explained.

"Sheriff, I am the Medical Examiner; I look at human corpses. I find the cause of death of humans, not animals. I'm afraid that I am not skilled in this area and will not be able to help you," the Medical Examiner responded.

The Sheriff replied, "I am well aware of your experience and training. I realize that this is out of the realm of your position, but it is not beyond your expertise. I know that you can refuse to do this, but I don't know what else to do. I do not know what we are dealing with or looking for. If you could just tell me what sort of animal, this could help direct our efforts."

The Sheriff's eyes were pleading with hers. Her biggest personal fault was that she had a hard time saying no. She often ended up burning the candle from both ends, a result of over-committing herself.

She looked again at the Sheriff's face before she said, "I don't know that I will be of any service, but I will at least take a look. Have one of your guys bring three of the recovered remains to my lab."

Chapter 32

Blythe Aspen was already regretting her decision to look at the dead animals even before she made it back to her vehicle. At least the Sheriff agreed to transport the corpses to her lab. She had all of her tools with her, she could have easily performed her task there on the spot, but this way she could address this on her own time – in between everything else she had going on.

Ms. Aspen stopped by her favorite Mexican restaurant on the way back to her office. Her lunch 'hour' lasted a mere 25 minutes, this included ordering and scarfing down her enchiladas, beans, and rice. Her iPhone began buzzing on her hip. She detached the unit that kept her accessible to the world. She glanced at the screen, a text message from her lab.

"Hey, Sheriff's Department is here trying to drop off the corpses of people's pets? The deputy is stating that you are expecting them. What do you want me to do?"

Blythe thought that the Sheriff was being pushy on this. She had not given Theresa the heads up about the animal corpses. Cutting her lunch short, she texted back:

"On my way. Have them put in the fridge for lab 3. I will take care of them later. Thanks."

Chapter 33

Malcolm was into his fourth night in the High Sierras. He found the perfect spot, far from any beaten path. He finished setting up camp by 4:00 pm, had an early dinner of spam and country gravy. Now he wandered with his camera to find signs of life.

He had scoped out a nice looking meadow during his travels, now about a mile away from his camp. He backtracked the way that he came. Once he found the meadow, he searched for any game trails.

He found one that crossed through the heart of the meadow and down to a rushing creek.

After examining the surrounding mountains, he made a prediction of which way the evening breezes would blow. He positioned himself downwind from the game trail.

There he sat. He watched as the sun dropped behind the high peak, casting a premature sunset across the valley where he resided. Within minutes, crickets and frogs began to sing their evening tunes. Birds chirped, and chipmunks chased each other up the trunks of large Jeffery pine trees.

Malcolm's stomach began to growl. He decided to wait just a bit longer and then head back to camp for another round of dinner. Just as he was debating on how much longer to wait, he saw a large doe poke her head out of the trees.

Malcolm froze in place. Willing even his hair to stay put.

The doe hesitantly scanned the meadow and then slowly moved out into the open. She took a few steps and then stopped. She twisted her ears and tilted her head. She was searching for any signs that she had been spotted. Content that no predator was around; she advanced into the meadow, drawing closer to the stream.

Another deer jumped into the meadow and followed the same track. Shortly after, a third deer joined the group.

The third deer was half the size of the first one. She looked to be a year or so old.

Malcolm waited for the deer to pass him on their way to the stream. His intention was to steal pictures of them drinking at the stream.

He waited, frozen and stiff as a statue. The deer passed so close that Malcolm could smell the dirty fur. The wind worked perfectly to prevent the deer from smelling him. He hid in the tall grass of the meadow, watching the deer move past him.

Once the third deer passed, they were finally all busily drinking. Malcolm snatched a few pictures while zooming in with his adjustable lens. He then carefully crept on all four to get a better vantage point. Moving closer to where the deer drank, he stopped anytime he made or heard a noise. The deer never gave any indication that they were aware of his presence.

Malcolm crouched to the ground and slowly honed in on the rumps of the deer. Their white tails stood erect and twitched as they quenched their thirst with fresh cold mountain stream water. The sound of the bubbling brook masked the minimal noise that Malcolm created.

Malcolm was now within leaping distance. He had forgotten all about his camera. Something had taken over. He felt a deep instinctual primal feeling growing from his gut. He could not advert his eyes from the white hindquarters of the largest deer.

His realized his mouth was watering, but he feared that slurping would risk the deer becoming aware of his presence.

He was now close enough that he could reach out and touch the deer.

The smallest of the deer raised her head and jumped away at the site of Malcolm. Malcolm's body leapt onto the closest doe. The third deer jumped across the stream in a single bound and darted off into the forest with a zigzag pattern.

The largest deer struggled to stay upright. It dragged its hind legs with Malcolm's mass weighing it down. The deer pulled at the dirt and rocks along the shoreline. It hopped, kicked, and struggled. The deer managed to crawl into the stream, dragging Malcolm along with it.

He had not thought about attacking the deer, but his body was on autopilot. He felt that he was a spectator, rather than a participant.

The deer fought to get away, but within seconds, Malcolm had wrestled the animal to submission. The doe collapsed into the shallow waters. Once the deer was on her side, Malcolm sunk his teeth into the jugular vein that ran down her neck. Malcolm chewed and sucked until the deer stopped moving.

Chapter 34

Malcolm dragged the deer back onto dry land. There he proceeded to rip away at the fur and devour the warm meaty flesh of his prize. He continued eating for about an hour. He pulled away at the deer, tearing away the fur from the meat. Repeatedly he sunk his face into the meat.

The warm, fresh, raw meat satisfied his cravings more than anything else that he had ever realized. At one point he noticed that he was humming as he ate. At that moment he seemed completely satisfied. He was happy to be alive. Never feeling so alive.

He lost track of time and became totally involved in devouring his feast. He failed to realize that the sun had set and dark shadows were taking over the valley floor.

Malcolm continued to eat, despite being bloated from the overindulgence. The only thing that caused him to stop was the unmistakable growl of something bigger than him, a black bear.

Frozen with his head buried into the inner thigh, Malcolm

determined the direction from which the growl had come. The hair on his neck stood at attention. He wondered the purpose for the hair to stand up when scared. He reasoned that this must somehow increase the human ability to detect threats. He wondered how long his hair had been trying to tell him that a bear now wanted to finish his meal.

He tried to determine the distance between where he was and where the bear was. He tried to look around without moving. All he could see was darkness.

Malcolm figured that his best bet was to slowly move away from the carcass in the opposite direction of the bear. He slowly backed away, heading up stream, keeping his face directed toward the growling.

It was not until this point that Malcolm realized that his shirt was covered in the deer's blood. Making him feel shrink-wrapped, the Mountain Hardware poly-blend shirt clung to his stomach.

When he was a fair distance from the bear, he could see the massive shadow meander out of the trees. The bear settled down next to the carcass and began to finish where Malcolm had left off.

Chapter 35

Jack was watching the Democratic National Convention while finishing his dinner and beer. He always made a point of watching both the Republican and Democratic conventions. He believed that the conventions demonstrated where the nation was headed, what to get excited about, and what to worry about.

Tessy was in another room; she couldn't stand listening to politicians. The fluctuations in their speeches bothered her. Every time she heard them speaking, she would inquire, "Why can't they just talk normal? Say what they have to say and get on with it. Instead of DUH, de, DUH, de, DUH."

She would state this while raising and lowering her arms, mimicking the men in suits.

The doorbell rang, followed by a solid four knocks on the door.

Jack muted the television and with an exhalation, raised himself off of the couch. As he approached the door, Tessy entered the room.

"Who's at the door?" Tessy asked as Jack made his way across the room.

Jack stopped and looked Tessy in the eyes with a face that clearly demonstrated that he could not believe that she was asking such a ridiculous question.

Tessy hated it when Jack made her feel silly for asking questions, especially ill-timed questions.

"It's the police," Jack said as he took a glance through the peephole.

"The police? What do they want?"

Jack turned and gave the look again as he twisted the knob and opened the door. Two police officers stood at attention on his front porch.

"What can I do for you guys?" Jack asked.

"Are you Jack Wilson?"

"Yes," Jack responded hesitantly.

Tessy sidled up behind Jack, a movement that suggested that she had his back.

"Sir, do you know a Julie Munger?"

"Julie Munger?" Jack thought out loud. He could not place the name.

"The name sounds familiar, but I am much better with faces than names. I never forget a face. Do you have a picture?"

"No, no we do not have a picture to show you."

"Ok, well, what is this about?"

"Mrs. Munger's child is missing. Your name came up in the discussion of the case."

"I'm sorry, I don't understand. Her child is missing and my name came up? How? Why? When?"

Tessy pushed up on the side of Jack.

"Officers, what is going on here? Is my husband in trouble? I can assure you that he is a good man."

"Ma'am, we just would like to ask your husband some questions."

Jack thought it over for a moment. He was having a hard time making sense of the matter.

"Officers, I'm sure that there has been some misunderstanding. Would you like to come inside? We have nothing to hide, please, come in. I'll answer your questions and do what I can to help."

"Jack, what are you doing?" Tessy whispered, though due to their proximity the officers heard her question.

"Tess, there is a child missing and these guys think we can help. Let's hear them out."

"We have done nothing wrong and what if you say something that makes them think otherwise?"

"Hon, not talking to them, not letting them in, and us bantering about this makes us look guilty. Please, just cooperate and everything will be fine."

"I'm not so sure," Tessy finished defiantly.

Chapter 36

"Let's sit at the dining room table," Jack invited the officers.

"Can I get you guys something to drink?" Jack offered.

"No, thanks." Both officers answered in unison.

After they were all seated the officer continued.

"So you say the name Julie Munger sounds familiar, but that you can not place the name with a face?"

"Yes, can you tell me where she lives," Jack inquired?

"No, we can't divulge specifics about the case. How do you know the Mungers?"

Jack instinctually gave the officer the same look he gave Tessy, but quickly withdrew the glare.

Jack asked, "What can you tell me? I'm cooperating here. I'm trying to help. But you are not giving me anything I can work with."

"Can you tell me where you were yesterday between noon and 6?"

Jack thought for a moment. It was obvious that the police considered him a suspect for a missing child. He did not want to make himself look guilty - but at the same time - he wished to help this child and family, if at all possible.

"I was here at home during that time," Jack responded matter of factly.

"Can anyone attest to this? Was your wife here? Maybe your neighbors saw you?"

"No, I was here alone. I wrenched my back and shoulders jackhammering all day Tuesday. So yesterday, I was taking it easy. I spent the day on the couch. I never left the house."

Tessy chimed in, "My husband was in pain yesterday. He never left the house. He was on the couch when I left for work and was still there – in the same clothes – when I got home."

Jack put a hand on Tessy's thigh. He knew that she tended to be hotheaded. He worried that she would do more harm than good in trying to defend him. As usual, Tessy paid no mind to Jack's attempt of calming her down.

"Ma'am, what time did you leave and what time did you return home?"

"I left for work at 7 and was home by 4:30."

"This leaves from noon to 4:30 unaccounted for," the officer deduced.

"I talked to Jack on my lunch break around 12:30. He was still home on the couch," Tessy offered.

"Ok, good. Did you call the house phone or his mobile," the officer inquired.

"His mobile, we do not have a landline," Tessy replied deflated.

"Ok, that is not too bad. We can secure the data from your service provider that will tell us where he was when he took your call. Who is your service through and what are your numbers?"

Jack responded, "We are with Verizon."

The second officer handed Jack his notepad and pen. Jack jotted down the numbers. Then the officer pulled out his phone and dialed a number while he stepped into the kitchen.

Chapter 37

Blythe pulled into the parking lot of the coroner's office as the Sheriff's van was pulling away. She continued to mutter under her breath about agreeing to perform autopsies on these pets. Sheriff Glasgow was a friend of her mother's and was largely responsible for Blythe landing this career. She was eternally grateful, but she wondered if the feelings of indebtedness would ever wear off. Anytime Glasgow asked a favor of her, she felt obligated to respond.

It had been a long time since Blythe had been in a biology lab, the last time she dissected an animal. Personally speaking, Blythe didn't like pets. Her pragmatic way of thinking couldn't grasp the point. She understood the value of companionship, the positive affection received from pets, but she didn't feel that these positive aspects were worth the cost.

In the mind of Blythe Aspen, pets were things. Blythe subscribed to the belief that one does not own things, things own you. A pet requires attention, requires feeding, looking after. She rolled her eyes every time somebody had to leave a party early to let a dog out. She knew of more than a few occasions when pet owners passed up on a trip because of their pets. It was because of these observances that Blythe developed the belief that pets weakened and confined a person.

She had many dinner discussions over her stance on pets. She also incorporated how pets and animals are responsible for nearly all diseases and sicknesses that ail mankind. The discussions would become so controversially heated that she soon learned to place the topic in the same category as religion and politics.

Chapter 38

It was with trepidation that Blythe Aspen entered her office, where a line of corpses, dead kitty's, and puppies awaited her attention. She was already behind schedule; the previous week had been unprecedented with homicides. She knew there was no point in asking for help; this was just a temporary flood of deaths that would hopefully let up soon.

Approaching the oversized glass door, Blythe paused long enough to examine her appearance in her reflection. It was a habit she had formed over the years and had saved her from more than one embarrassing situation. Once, in her haste to get to work, she had somehow managed to leave the house without addressing her shoulder length hair. She was known for having her hair perfect, not one strand out of place. The reflection as she approached the building afforded her the opportunity to rush back to her Mercedes before anyone was the wiser.

Blythe smoothed out her dress, and pulled out her magnetized key card. She waived the card a few times over the square box beside the door, until she received a green light accompanied by the familiar 2-second tone and the clicking of the door unlocking.

She pulled the door toward her and stepped inside where she performed the same ritual for the second door. The amount of security over dead bodies always amused her.

As she entered into the lobby of her home-away-from-home, she was greeted with a hello from the front desk receptionist, Trish.

"The animals are in the fridge in Lab 3 as you requested. What gives with the animals? Are we even allowed to have dead animals in here?"

Blythe responded, "Please, don't ask. I don't know how I get myself into these things."

Trish could see the stress level expressed on the face of Blythe. She offered her support and asked if there was anything she could do.

Blythe yelled as she was walking down the hall, "Yeah, teach me how to say no to people."

Chapter 39

Blythe entered the women's bathroom, relished the pause in her day as she relieved herself in the 'privacy' of one of the three stalls. She contemplated how long she could sit there before someone checked on her or her phone started buzzing.

As if on cue, her phone began the persistent nagging buzz of a giant mosquito. The phone was even more annoying as it vibrated against the side of the porcelain fixture.

She sighed as she looked at the caller ID. The Sheriff could wait, at least long enough to afford her the privacy of a bio-break. Awe, who was she kidding? She answered the phone on the fourth ring.

"Aspen."

The Sheriff chimed in, "Blythe, what do you think about the corpses?"

"Sorry Sheriff, haven't had a chance to look at them just yet. I am completely swamped here and with all due respect, the animals do not take precedence. I will look at them as soon as I can."

The Sheriff replied, "Blythe, I know you are swamped, we all are constantly swamped. That's the nature of the beast when working in the public sector. I realize that you are doing me a favor, and I don't mean to be pushy, but something is going on here and I'd like to find out. With your experience and trained eye, it won't take you but a few minutes to glance at the corpses and let me know what you think."

Sharply Dr. Aspen responded, "David, I will get to them as soon as I can and then I will call you, alright!"

With the end of her declaration, Blythe stood and flushed the toilet. She intentionally used his first name, just as she intentionally held her earpiece over the swirling toilet to capture the unmistakable gushing-swirling sound that only commercial toilets could make.

Blythe opened the stall to find Trish looking back at her with a concerned look on her face. Blythe returned the look with one free of sympathy. Trish's mouth began to twitch instances before she broke into a full-blown laugh. The women did not have to exchange words; they fully understood each other.

Blythe washed her hands and then pulled her lab coat from her locker. Trish reminded Blythe that she had to leave early today to pick her cat up from the Vet.

Blythe responded, "Yes, of course, no sense in both of us staying late."

What she was thinking was something completely different.

Chapter 40

After all that they had gone through with the intruder, the last thing Cammie wanted to do was go to the annual family reunion. She loved the family, but they could be overwhelming. She fought Seth on this trip, but he insisted that it would be good to get away from the house.

Seth argued, "Fresh Air will do us good and we can really use the support of the family right now. Besides, we were already packed and ready to go, before..."

Seth let his sentence trail off. They were all trying to forget what had happened.

Cammie agreed they had to get away. The kids were scared, she was scared, and the neighbors continued to bombard them with concern. They did already have the trip planned, so she conceded.

The Parker family reunion happened every year at the same location. It began when the family consisted of 5 members. Grandma and Grandpa Parker loved family and found their purpose in life through them. They decided to continue having kids and soon had a family of seven children. Now they were all grown, married, and raising their own. The Parkers now had 23 grandchildren and a great grandchild on the way.

The Parkers bought a small cabin in the Sierra Nevada Mountain Range, just outside of Yosemite National Park. The annual gathering tradition began as soon as their children began their own lives. Over the years the men of the family added new cabins and structures to the property. They affectionately referred to the place as the Parker Commune. The property now consisted of 5 cabins, a baseball diamond, a bocce ball court, volleyball, horseshoes, and a man-made pond. The family purchased a large 100-year-old barn from the Fresno area and relocated it to the property.

They reconstructed and refurbished the structure. When they finished, the barn was a finished building with plumbing, electrical, flooring, and insulated from the elements. It became the favorite gathering spot on the property. The hayloft was converted into a large sleeping area for the kids. The main floor had a large projection screen for movies, a pool table, skee, tennis, a kitchen, two baths and two bedrooms. A large fireplace heated the barn, hand built by the brothers with stones they recovered from the land. They wanted an old fashioned fireplace, the kind that one could walk into and stand up in. They built benches around the inside of the large firebox that allowed for the kids to sit and roast marshmallows or warm their toes after playing in the snow.

Though Cammie really did not want to be around anybody, her spirit lifted as they drove higher in elevation and deeper into the forest. The smell of pine trees always cheered her up. She began to agree with her husband, that going to the family reunion was just what they needed.

Chapter 41

Every morning Jonathan performed the same ritual. His alarm
clock would go off at 5:55, set to the local news station. He would
lie in bed and listen to the traffic report, mentally preparing for his
commute. Then he would make his way to the kitchen for his
Keurig coffee, on the way flipping on the flat screen on the wall to
continue his morning fix of news and financial updates. After
finishing his coffee, Jonathan usually went for a morning run
followed by his ritualistic showering, grooming, and dressing
ceremony.

As soon as the alarm clock went off, Jonathan knew the world was
changing. Interrupting the traditional traffic report was the sound
of the EAS (Emergency Alert System). Jonathan always
wondered if the multiple testing of the system would desensitize
people from actually tuning in during a real disaster. He noticed
with colleagues and friends that as soon as the annoying signal
began broadcasting, people would either change the station or
turn down the volume until the sound ceased. Having been raised
in a family that respected the predictions of Revelations and
prepared for the Apocalypse, Jonathan always forced himself to
pay attention to the annoying EAS signal. He feared the effects of

becoming desensitized.

Jonathan lay wide eyed in the dark of his bedroom, concentrating his sense of hearing on the sound radiating from his alarm clock radio. The signal was interrupted periodically by an announcement, "This is not a test. This is not a test. The EAS signal that you are hearing will momentarily be followed by a press release from the Center for Disease Control. Please stay tuned for the following important message." Jonathan felt his heart beat increase, something big was happening.

Jumping out of bed and rushing for the television remote, Jonathan pressed the "All On" button. The color on the name decal of the TV was the first to show any sign of receiving the signal from the remote. The red-orange sleep mode changed to a bright blue as the TV warmed up. Jonathan hated this delaying sequence of modern technology.

He missed his old box TV from his college days. The old TV would come alive as soon as the power button was pulled. He cursed the government every time he turned on the boob tube. He was forced to "upgrade" when the FCC was persuaded to do away with the analog signals for television broadcasting.

He wrote letters to his representatives and signed petitions. Thinking to himself, "when has writing your congressperson ever worked?"

The government promised conversion boxes for citizens who desired to keep their analog televisions. Jonathan requested the conversion box on the first day that they were taking request. He was disappointed when he heard the report that they had grossly underestimated the amount of people who would want to keep their televisions and therefore only had a limited supply of the boxes.

Jonathan never received his box, nor did he know of anyone who ever did. Among his fellow conspiracy theorist in his Yahoo group, discussions ranged from the boxes never existed to the few boxes that were sent out never worked properly.

Jonathan was forced to purchase a new digital television and did so the day that his prehistoric roof mounted antennae could no longer produce a picture. As always, he performed the research prior to making his purchase. He reviewed Consumer Reports and read personal reviews online. He felt confident when he made the purchase.

Two months later he cursed the government as he returned the television for having problems with the screen. He despised government officials who coward to lobbyist. He blamed the whole analog-to-digital fiasco on corporate greed, manipulating government.

The sales rep told him that many people were experiencing problems with burned out pixels or TVs that would not turn on/off. The word on the street was that the life expectancy of the new technology was 2-5 years. He shook his head as he thought of the old television his parents still possessed. The one he grew up watching.

His parents still preferred to watch videos on the old boob tube. His father refused to pay for cable or satellite. He felt it depicted the greed in society. Charging customers for television reception and then subjecting them to watch commercials as well – was an out right crime, his father often preached.

Jonathan longed for his old analog.

About one year from the big push for digital televisions, Jonathan began to notice a change in reviews for the appliances. Many consumers were experiencing frustrations with the technology. Frustrations that was fueled by companies with limited warrantees and impossible to deal with customer relations. Jonathan was "lucky," his fifth digital television purchase was still going strong after 4 years. He prided himself for giving up on paying the price for a new TV, instead deciding to purchase a *refurbished*. His argument for doing so was that the problems have been discovered and fixed – he was right.

Finally, the television came to life and the cable signal was found. Now with his freshly brewed coffee in hand, Jonathan sat on the edge of his sofa and waited for the broadcast.

Chapter 42

Jonathan watched as the news broadcasters discussed the upcoming press conference.

"Speculations of a world wide epidemic maybe the reason for this immediate call for a press conference on the part of the Center for Disease Control. Our sources have made telephone calls to both the CDC and the White House. So far, no reports or communication is available. It is as if the capital is on lock down. Again, we are urging everyone to stay tuned to the following message. This is unprecedented."

His female counterpart interrupted, "Yes, typically we are given a heads' up as to the topic of relevance. We usually have something to offer to our listeners, but at the moment, we are waiting in anticipation and asking that you do the same."

Jonathan blindly reached for his MacBook Pro. As soon as he flipped open the lid the laptop sprung to life.

At least some companies have gotten it right, he thought to himself.

He logged onto his Yahoo chat room. As predicted, the group was excited and plugging up the conversation with theories and conjectures. Postings consisted of everything from Alien invasions to a Zombie Apocalypse.

For the most part, Jonathon enjoyed the banter. He loved the entertainment value of conspiracy theorist. But this morning he hoped that somebody had enough intelligence to discuss what was happening.

As he perused his computer screen, his focused ear picked up on the news anchor's voice.

"I'm standing here in the conference room, waiting for the CDC spokesperson. We have just been told that we will be addressed shortly. They have not told us who will be addressing us. But who will be addressing us, will not be as important as what they will be saying."

Jonathan rolled his eyes; everything seemed to be such a production. *Just tell us what we need to know so we can get on with our days,* he thought to himself as he sipped his coffee that was now getting cold. He stood up and walked to the kitchen to nuke his 'mug of Joe.' As soon as he pressed the start button, he heard the television go silent; the silence either meant another technological interruption or that the speaker had taken to the stage.

Jonathan interrupted the nuking process and pulled out his lukewarm coffee and headed back into the family room. He stopped in mid-stride, coffee poised before his mouth, eyes fixed on the television. At the podium, with the CDC emblem behind him was the President of the United States of America.

What?...Why?... How?... Jonathan was having difficulty even beginning to form any questions. Where to start? What was the

President doing at a CDC press conference? If the President is addressing the Nation, why not just call a press conference under the realm of the Presidency? What is going on?

"My fellow Americans" the President began.

Chapter 43

The words acted as a release mechanism that broke the trance Jonathan was stuck in. He realized that he had frozen in mid-stride with the coffee millimeters away from the intended target. He took a swig as he lowered himself back onto the couch.

He glanced at his computer screen. He had a number of chat invitations from buddies. All of the bubbles had similar messages.

"POTUS at the CDC?"

"CDC and the Prez? What is going on?"

"A biological warfare experiment went haywire in New Mexico, no doubt"

The President continued, "I come before you as we end the summer season and move into fall, to remind you of another season that has come early this year. The season that I speak of is the Flu Season.

"Many of us do not give enough serious attention to the Flu Virus, even though it kills many people every year. This year, the World

Health Organization and the CDC are predicting a devastating flu season. Therefore, I come before you to urge each of you to have yourselves and your loved ones vaccinated as soon as possible. There is plenty of vaccine available; there is no shortage and no need to panic. But the sooner we all obtain this vaccination the better protected we will all be.

"I have already spoken with members of Congress in conjunction with members of CDC and FEMA to assure that everyone has access to the necessary vaccine. The vaccine is being made available to everyone without cost. Doctors and pharmacies will be reimbursed for the cost of providing the vaccines. Under the advisement of health officials, I am imposing an in juncture on the nasal method of delivering the vaccine. The method releases a live virus into the nose and poses a threat for this particular flu-season. We are urging everyone to receive the injection version of the vaccine which is a "dead-virus" and therefore less likely for someone to come down with the flu and continue spreading the virus.

"To demonstrate my support and the importance of obtaining this vaccine, I will be rolling up my sleeve and receiving the injection before you today. Nancy?"

The President turned to his right and a woman approached the President. She helped him remove his jacket and rolled up his sleeve. He then returned his attention to the cameras and smiled. Another person walked up beside Nancy with a silver tray.

After swabbing the President's arm with alcohol, Nancy picked up a syringe and bottle of vaccine. She carefully inserted the syringe into the vial, drew the liquid, and removed the syringe. She tapped the syringe, removed the air, pinched the President's arm and gingerly inserted the needle.

The President's face never changed, not even a hint of a squirm. The needle was removed, a cotton ball secured, and then the woman named Nancy handed the President a small yellow sucker. The audience of news reporters began chuckling.

Upon the return of his suit jacket, the President continued, "You see; that was not so bad. Please, my fellow Americans, I urge you all to not delay in obtaining the vaccine. Thank you for your time. May we all have a healthy winter this year. Thank you and God Bless."

With that, the President raised his hand and waived as he walked off the stage. He paid no attention to the audience of reporters shouting out questions. Camera flashes filled the air. The news anchor appeared back onto the screen.

"We have just heard from the President of the United States of America in a surprising visit to the CDC, where he apparently received an injection of the flu vaccine. It is a surprising maneuver by the President and the Health Organization to get the message out. Making use of the Emergency Alert System is bound to cause a stir by opponents of the President. I am Maggie Thurgood at the headquarters for the CDC, back to you Charles."

Jonathan sat in disbelief as he stared at the screen. How weird was that? He recounted what had just happened, the EAS was released – effectively interrupting all broadcasting on radio and television stations nationwide. The EAS was reserved for times of emergencies only. How was an invitation to obtain the flu vaccine an emergency?

Next, the public was made to wait for the broadcast to begin. The only hint given was that the broadcast was to take place at the CDC. Surprisingly the message is delivered from the President. Instead of addressing an emergency, the President preaches a social lesson on the importance of the flu vaccine.

The conspiracy theorist inside Jonathon's head was racing with possibilities.

Perhaps the flu vaccine carried a hidden property that will allow the government to track everybody. Maybe the labs that predict and develop the vaccines accidently created a devastating strain that has the potential to wipe out mankind. More than likely, the lobbyist convinced the President to perform this stunt to raise sales of their product and thus maximize profits for their shareholders, Jonathan settled.

Chapter 44

The bear devoured what remained of the deer. Malcolm listened as the beast crunched bones with his powerful jaws. He could hear the tearing sound as his sharp claws tore into the hide.

Malcolm thought he should take pictures of this, but worried that the flash would irritate the bear. He absent-mindedly raised his hand to the camera that hung around his neck. The camera was not there.

Where is my camera?

Malcolm had a moment of panic as he attempted to retrace his steps. The whole stalking and attack on the deer was now a distant fog. It did not feel that it was he that performed the deed. It now seemed like a distant story that he had once heard.

He could not remember dropping or placing the camera down. He could not risk heading back to look for it now; the bear would assume him a threat. No, he would have to return in the morning.

Malcolm began stumbling his way back toward his camp. As he

walked, his blood soaked skin and clothes chilled him to the bone. He then realized the stench that followed him. Knowing that he could not climb into his sleeping bag covered in blood, he turned back toward the stream.

The stream was fresh snowmelt and the cool night breeze was numbing. Malcolm stripped off all of his clothes and began soaking them in the river. He beat them against rocks. After an excruciating period of time, Malcolm's fingers and toes were too numb to be any good. His body was shivering, and he still needed to rinse off his blood stained skin.

He forced himself into the stream and vigorously scrubbed down his body with his opened hands. His hands were so numb that it felt as if somebody else was touching him. He quickly exited the stream and resolved that the cleaning would have to suffice until he could perform a better job under the warming sun.

Malcolm made his way back to camp in the dark, trying to imagine where he had lost his Black Diamond headlamp.

"It's probably laying next to the camera", he said sarcastically to himself.

Back at camp, he lowered his bag from the tree, where he kept it out of harm's reach. Blindly he felt along his bag to the top lid and unzipped the top pocket. He dug inside and pulled out his backup flashlight/glow stick. He pushed in the button and the light instantly displayed his surroundings.

He next made his way to his tent, unzipped the flap door, and pulled out the long underwear that he had stashed on top of his Agnes Sleeping bag. He pulled the tight fitting fabric over his damp skin. The cold damp skin made the task difficult as it grabbed at the fabric.

Once he had the underwear covering his skin, he then reached into the tent and pulled out his puffy down jacket. The shell that encompassed the goose feathers was cold to the touch, but Malcolm knew from experience that the jacket would trap his heat and be cozy within a couple of minutes.

Finishing the ensemble, Malcolm pulled a night man's cap over his head. He still remembered the lesson he learned as a young Boy Scout; "80 percent of your body heat escapes from your head. If you're cold, put a hat on." He could still hear the voice of wisdom being passed on from his Scoutmaster.

Still shivering, Malcolm returned to his pack. He pulled out his Jet Boil and fired it up with a cup of water. While he waited for the water to boil, he turned his attention to his campfire.

The fire was already built; it just needed to be lit. Malcolm had a system when he arrived at a new place to camp: set up the tent/shelter, gather firewood for the night, cook a meal/snack, and figure out a secure place for the food. There was no time for relaxing until these tasks were completed. This regiment had paid off more than once, tonight was no exception.

Frozen to the core, Malcolm was in no shape to begin searching for wood or constructing a fire. No, instead, he simply pressed the trigger on his lighter and touched it to the petroleum cubes he had strategically placed among the kindling.

The fire slowly took on life. Malcolm got down low, next to the fighting flame. He offered slow, long, breaths; breathing life into the flame. The kindling took, and soon the flame grew. He continued to blow oxygen. Each puff of air resulted in the sound of a small roar as his oxygen increased the power of the growing flame.

The kindling burned and passed the growing flames onto the larger lumber. The twigs, branches, and pinecones crackled. The flames grew and began producing heat. Instantly, Malcolm's mood improved. He allowed the glow and warmth of the fire to engulf him. He finally began to relax, the shivering changing from a constant annoyance to a periodic sputter.

The water was rolling as it came to a full boil. Malcolm reached over and turned the knob to squelch the flame. He poured the hot liquid into his squishy cup and added hot cocoa with a splash of Jameson whisky from his plastic flask.

The hot alcoholic beverage raced down his insides. He could feel the warmth spread from his core outward. The fire warmed him from the outside in, while his beverage quickly covered the distance from the inside out.

Malcolm allowed himself to relax, enjoying the warmth, he reflected on the day's events. He fathomed over his ability to take down a wild animal with his bare hands. How was he able to sneak up so close, undetected. He contemplated how it seemed that some part of him –previously unaware of- had taken over. Was this a primitive trait, left over from distant ancestors? What possessed him to attack the deer and to eat it raw?

As he lay there next to the fire, his back up against his backpack, he turned his head heavenward. Out of habit, he found Orion's belt, the middle star – and his thoughts turned to the love of his life. He wondered what Brenda was doing at that moment.

Most likely she was out on the back deck, wrapped in a blanket, drinking wine, and staring at the very same star.

Either that or she was online examining his latest Spot reporting. Crap! The Spot! When was the last time I pushed the button? Shit, she had probably already sent out the cavalry to rescue me. Damn it! How could I be so stupid?

Malcolm clawed at his backpack. The Spot was his least favorite item to carry, along with the GPS unit that his wife insisted on him taking. He kept both of them deep at the bottom of his pack.

His hand dug around, searching for the familiar hard plastic and ribbed sides of the handheld device. He meant to check it earlier to make sure that the device had coverage in this little valley. He fired it up and pushed the "I'm ok" button. The device began searching for a signal.

Chapter 45

Brenda sat on her back deck, wrapped in a blanket, and enjoying her red wine. The glow of her MacBook screen illuminated her face. She continually checked the Spot website, waiting for an updated signal.

This was the second night that Malcolm had failed to communicate. The last time was close to where he indicated on his map that he would be going off-trail.

She hated him going backpacking by himself, but even more so, she hated him going off trails.

What was he thinking? She thought. *What was his obsession with the outdoors and being alone, not just alone, but really alone? Was something wrong with him?*

Malcolm had made several attempts of explaining his expeditions to her, but she never quite understood. He wasn't exactly an introvert. He liked being around their friends, hanging out, going for drinks, and dancing the night away. He could party and socialize with the best of them. So why did he insist on going alone into the woods?

She contemplated on how long she should give him before reporting him lost.

She knew he hated the tethering of the Spot, but each time he reported that he was 'ok,' she felt reassured. She was literally a wreck until she received his phone call that he was out of the woods and had stopped for his traditional burger and fries in Oakdale.

She could not sleep. She bounced between checking the Spot website and her Facebook page. Her girlfriend, Pamela, was awake as well, having ended her shift as a nurse at Mt. Diablo Hospital. Her fluctuating schedule made it difficult for her to sleep at night. They had been chatting for the past 30 minutes. She sent her another message.

"I don't know how long I should wait before calling the Ranger Station."

"Knowing Malcolm, he is enjoying himself in the middle of nowhere. He probably has lost track of time. Most likely, he is out of the service area. Those things are only helpful if three satellites can see you."

"I know, but I can not help picturing him with a twisted ankle or stuck under a boulder like Aron Ralston. He could be sipping on his urine as we speak! He could be sitting there, waiting for me to make the call to send someone out to save him."

"He is such a dimwit for putting you through this every year! If he wasn't so good to you the rest of the year, I'd tell you to ditch his ass."

"Ha, Ha."

"He's resourceful and knows what he's doing. Don't worry. He'll be fine."

"Seriously, how long should I wait?"

"How long has it been?"

"The last time he checked in was two nights ago. He agreed to at least once a day."

"Ok, if you don't hear from him by noon tomorrow, call it in."

Chapter 46

"Can you at least tell me why my name came up? Did this Julie Munger tell you how she knows me? Or why I am a suspect?"

Jack desperately tried to piece the nonsense together. He could only imagine what must be going through Tessy's head.

The first officer continued, "Sir, what do you do for a living?"

"I'm a General Contractor. I remodel kitchens and baths."

The officer gave him a look that revealed the connection. Jack was perceptive to the clue.

"So she knows me through my business? Did I work on her place?"

The officer said nothing. He sat there waiting for his partner and allowed Jack to mull over the information in his head.

"Honey, would you get me my MacBook, please?"

Tessy left the room and within seconds returned with the laptop.

Jack spun the closed computer and flipped up the screen. The glowing signature Macintosh Apple glowed behind the skin of a moon lit landscape that was applied to the lid.

The screen instantly came to life. Jack navigated through his company files with ease. He clicked on the finder, scrolled down to select his company file, and then moved the cursor over the client folders. He slowed the movement when he came across the last names beginning with the letter M. Then he located the folder of the Munger's. He clicked and in the next column to the right, several files opened up. Estimates, notes, invoices, and change orders. He clicked on the first of the estimates. It popped up. Once he saw the address, his memory returned.

"Oh! Ok. I remember them now. The Mungers, they live in Alamo and have two little girls?"

"Yes, they live in Alamo, but they have two girls and a boy. I wouldn't call the girls little though," the Officer said while giving a doubtful glare.

The Officer wondered if this had all been a game for Jack. Was he pretending not to know this family? Was he hiding something? The officer watched Jack and Tessy closely for any tale-tell signs. He was nervous when Tessy left the room to fetch the computer. He was ready with one leg propped and a hand on his weapon for when she returned. He did not know if she would return with a computer or a gun. He wished for his partner to hurry back into the room. He was relieved when she produced the laptop.

"No? Oh, well I remodeled their kitchen several years ago." Jack referenced his records. "Yes, it has been 5 or 6 years. So the girls must be... teenagers?! Wow, how time flies. But when I worked for them, they did not have a son."

"The Munger's took on their Nephew when Julie's sister died."

"Oh, how terrible. Well, he is in good hands. The Munger's are good people. Those girls were so cute. I don't remember their names, but which one is missing?"

The officer again wondered if Jack was playing him. He seemed sincere, but it could still be an act.

"The younger girl is missing. When was the last time you saw the girls or had contact with the Mungers?"

"Gosh, I would say that I haven't seen them in 5 years or so, since I finished the work on their place. Oh, wait, I did see the older girl shortly after that. She was with a group of girls at a birthday party, at the rock gym where I climb."

"Did you say anything to her?"

"She recognized me, ran up, gave me a hug, and said, 'hello."

"Was her mother there?"

"No, she was with a bunch of girls and a few ladies that I did not know. A couple of Mom's were wondering who I was and obviously concerned. After she said hello, she ran back to the group and that was it."

"What was your relationship with the girls?"

"WHAT DO YOU MEAN? WHAT ARE YOU IMPLYING?" Tessy jumped to the defense of her husband.

"Tess, it's ok. He's just doing his job. This girl could be in danger. He just needs to clear me from his list of suspects, Right?" Jack turned his head and directed the question to the officer.

"That's right. If we can clear your husband from our list, we can narrow our focus in the right direction."

Jack understood and he was not offended. Tessy loved her husband and knew that he would never hurt a child. He didn't have it in him.

"While I was working on their place, the girls took a liking to me, especially the younger one. I love to joke and play around with kids; I enjoy being around them. The girls often would check on the work, ask me questions, or just watch. I was always chasing them out of the work area so they wouldn't get hurt. That was the full extent of the relationship."

"Did you ever give them gifts, talk to them on the phone, or were you ever left alone with them?"

Jack wanted to be open and honest. He tried to remember if any of this had occurred.

"I have been known to give candy to kids of my clients. I don't eat the stuff, so I pass it on to kids whenever I get it. I never talked to them on the phone. There may have been a time when Mrs. Munger left her children with me at home while she ran an errand, it isn't uncommon for a client to do so."

Jack and Tessy worried if being completely open with the officers would wind up biting them in their proverbial butts.

Chapter 47

"What else can you tell me about the Mungers and your relationship with them?"

"While I was working on the place, I'd say that I became close with the family. It happens all the time. I'll spend a few months working on a place and in that time, I bond with the family. It get's depressing when I finish a job, because I know that I may never see them again. Part of the job, I guess.

"The Mungers were no exception. I worked on their place for over six months. I was there in the mornings when the girls left for school, and there when they came home. They would often share their afternoon snacks with me.

"Oh, and I remember their dog. Their dog loved me as well. They had this expensive designer dog. He was so protective of the girls, very cute. They had problems with his obedience. I worked with him on my lunch breaks and taught him a few tricks. Julie was extremely pleased.

"So, how did my name come up?"

"Your name came up when we asked Mrs. Munger to give us names of anyone she could think of who showed any interest in her children."

Jack nodded his head. He loved children, but it always made parents nervous. He understood, a white man with no children, taking specific interest in their child, he'd be nervous as well. That is when he could tell if they were good parents.

"Those girls were cute, I adored them. I would never do anything to hurt them and I will do anything I can to help."

"My husband loves children and I'm always telling him to tone his attention down. It makes mothers anxious. He is such a sweet, kind-hearted man. He has a ton of nieces and nephews and he is just a big kid. He likes to play and joke. He takes an interest in other children because we haven't been able to have children of our own, until now."

Tessy stroked her open hands over her belly, smoothing her blouse and pulling it tight to reveal the baby bump.

"Congratulations, I hadn't realized. How far along are you?"

"We are four months now."

"I am very happy for you folks."

Chapter 48

The second officer returned from the kitchen.

"The story checks out. We confirmed that you were within 5 miles of your home when you took the call from your wife. The call took place at 12:23 and lasted 4 minutes."

The first officer scribbled the information on his notepad where he was constructing a timeline.

"Is there anything else that you can offer us to fill in the gap from 12:27 to when your wife came home? I want to believe you, I really do. But there is enough time there for you to drive out to Alamo, snatch the girl, and return home with time to spare."

Jack tried to think of something to offer up as an alibi. He had been completely cooperative, maybe too cooperative. He knew that he looked prime for being a suspect.

The officer tried to spell it out for Jack. He turned to his partner.

"How long would it take to drive from here to Alamo?"

"Thirty minutes, twenty if you pushed it."

"So conceivably, a person could drive there and back in forty minutes."

"Oh, sure they could. Just hop on 680, with no traffic, a little weaving, and you're there in no time. Going 80 plus, you could be there in 15."

"So, Jack, listen. I like you. I do not figure you for being a guy who would do a thing like this. But, I'll be honest with you; right now, it is not looking good for you. Unless you can come up with an alibi…" The cop raised his hands and shrugged his shoulders, demonstrating that this was beyond his control.

The second cop spoke up, "Look, you took an interest in the girls, you had a motive, you had the time, the ability, and no alibi. This is not looking good my friend."

Jack knew what the officers were saying. He did not appreciate them laying it on so thick. He was not an idiot; he saw the writing on the wall. He looked over at his lovely wife. Tess' face was wrought with worry. Was this how it ended? He had put his wife through so much lately, with the incident at the grocery store and him losing his mind. Now was he leaving her to raise their child alone? This could not be how their lives played out. He had to figure this out. Was he being framed? By whom? Was this a lesson from God? Why was this happening to them?

"Ok, Jack. I'm gonna level with you. We do not have enough to arrest you, but at this time, you are our primary suspect. So what we are going to do is ask you to come down to the station with us where we can continue this discussion."

Chapter 49

Jack could not get the words out of his mouth, so he simply nodded in compliance. He pictured himself down at the station, in the interrogation room for hours.

He thought to himself, *my life is really going through the ringer right now.*

Jack stared at the screensaver jumping around on the screen of his MacBook. He played through the events of the day before, trying to come up with something to offer.

Why, of all days, did I decide to stay home yesterday? A day full of nothing; nothing but laying on the couch stuffing my face while watching movies and searching the web. MOVIES AND THE WEB!

"WAIT! I ordered a movie. I can show you, on our account that I ordered and watched a movie yesterday. I was watching the movie when Tess called me, I paused and then continued after the call."

Jack pulled up their Comcast account on his computer. He pulled up the account history and in less than a minute, he showed the officers that he had ordered and watched his favorite movie, "The Big Fish."

"Jack, this is a good try, but frankly, it doesn't fly. You could have ordered the movie, let it play while you were gone. We have no way of confirming if you actually were here or not."

Jack was getting desperate.

"What about my Fastrak? I can show that I did not cross any bridges yesterday by calling up my Fastrak account."

The Fastrak was the device that many Californians used to pay tolls instead of stopping and paying with cash at a tollbooth. The account would provide a record of each time the transponder passed by the tollbooths.

"Sorry Jack, you could have anticipated the alibi and left the transponder at home. You could have simply paid with cash to avoid detection."

"What about email or Facebook," Tess offered. "Did you get on your email or Facebook yesterday?"

Jack thought about it. Yeah, sure he did, but did he post anything?

"I was on Facebook, but I do not know what time it was or if I even posted anything. Would you mind if I checked?"

"No, sure, go ahead."

Jack's finger brushed across the mouse pad and his screen jumped alive. He clicked on the Firefox emblem at the bottom of his screen. His Bloomberg homepage took the place of his desktop wallpaper. Within seconds he was logged into his Facebook page.

He scrolled through his messages and then leaned back with a smile on his face. There on his page was a post recorded at 1:15pm,

"Stuck at home with a sore back and bored out of my mind. This getting old shit really sucks."

The officer read the post, looked at the time and then added, "That's better, but it still doesn't completely fill the gap until your wife returned home."

Jack pulled up various comments that he had left on his friends' pages. The comments were spaced periodically throughout the day. He was bored out of his mind and continually logged on to see what was going on. From 2:00 to 3:15 he had an ongoing discussion with his cousin Jill.

The cop was satisfied. "Ok, looks like you have been saved by Facebook," he said with a smile.

His partner interjected, "Wait a minute. You could've done all this while on the road through your smartphone."

Jack countered, "No, if it was through my phone it would show on Facebook as coming from my phone."

Jack pulled up a message that he had sent from his phone. It showed that it had come from his phone as he had stated.

The officers looked at each other and nodded.

Tessy grabbed Jack's forearm and rested her head on his shoulder. They were both relieved that the cops finally believed them.

Chapter 50

Though Jack was relieved that he was off of the hook, he felt for the Mungers and the missing girl. He wanted to help. He prayed that the girl was alright.

"Can you think of anyone who would want to hurt the girls, the Mungers, or showed an interest in the girls?"

Jack thought long and hard. It was so long ago, and he only really saw the girls at their home.

"There is only one guy that I can think of, but it is a long shot. I really do not think he would do anything. I'd hate to give you his name and piss him off. I don't even know why I'm thinking about him, but he's the only one."

"Well, tell us about this guy and we'll decide if it is worth looking into. We'll keep your name out of it."

"Well, alright. I use to sub contract out my plumbing to this guy, John. He knew his trade well. I didn't care for the guy, hard to get along with. But he was a dang good plumber.

"Anyways, he hated that kids took a liking to me and not him. He was a big, dirty, grease bag. My clients would always complain about him. He looked dirty and talked dirty. I finally stopped using him, wasn't worth the hassle.

"But, a few times, he caused problems by telling my clients to be careful with me around their kids. He was careful never to make accusations, just said enough to make the women anxious.

"I'm not sure how many times he did this, but I know of at least two times. I had a good relationship with both of those clients, and they told me what he was saying to them. This was the main reason why I stopped subbing out to him."

"Do you have his contact information?"

"Yes, in fact, I'll get you his card."

Jack walked down the hall, into his office, and pulled John's business card from a stack of cards he kept in a drawer. He returned and handed the card over.

"Again, I really do not think that John would be the type of guy to hurt a child, but I would feel awful if it was him and I did not say anything," Jack stated.

"We understand. We'll keep you out of the conversation we have with him.

"Here is my card, if you think of anything else, give me a call."

"Sure. And if there is anything we can do to help, please let us know. Could you let Julie know that our prayers are with her and her family? We sincerely hope that the girl is found safe and alright."

"Yes, of course. We'll relay the message. You folks have a good evening. We are sorry for the interruption. Thanks for understanding and cooperating. We'll let you know if there are any further questions. Good night."

Chapter 51

Malcolm stressed about the signal not making it from the Spot device. He pictured Brenda at home, unable to sleep and fret with worry.

There was nothing that he could do until the morning. As soon as the sun came up, he would return to where he had attacked the deer and find his camera and headlamp. Then he would hike out of the valley and find a peak where he could obtain reception. Hopefully, he could accomplish this task before his wife called the Ranger Station.

Malcolm's mind wandered as he stared into the glowing embers of the fire.

He did not understand what was happening to him.

What had become of me? I am killing and eating pets and wild animals. It seems so primitive and barbaric. What will happen if I am ever caught?

Malcolm allowed his brain to imagine him locked up in a mental institution.

What would that do to Brenda? Maybe I should just stay out here, disappear. She would be sad and miss me for a while, but she would eventually move on. She could then find somebody normal; somebody who she did not have to question around their friends' animals.

He now knew that he could survive, simply by hunting with his bare hands. He imagined himself stealing hunting rifles and food - at night - from drunken hunters. He could live out there for the rest of his life. It would be better, for everyone.

He absolutely loved Brenda. He wanted her to remember who he was, not who he had become.

He fell asleep, having made the decision that come morning, he would not check in with the Spot.

Chapter 52

Tessy was not so sure that this was a good idea, but her husband insisted on delivering a casserole to the Munger's. He wanted to demonstrate to them that there were not any hard feelings for them giving his name to the authorities. He also wanted to offer his support in their time of need. Tessy thought it was best to leave them alone, but she knew that he would do this with or without her, so she conceded in supporting him.

Tessy's heart was beating faster than she thought it should. She did not know why she was so nervous; all they were doing was delivering food to a family who was missing a child.

Jack knocked on the door and waited. Then he reached across Tessy and rang the bell. Nobody answered the door.

Jack decided to leave the casserole on one of the chairs that resided on the porch. He slid the Hallmark card under one of the corners of the dish. He painstakingly searched for the right card, but resolved on a blank card.

I guess Hallmark doesn't exactly make cards for families with missing children, Jack had thought to himself while staring at the many categories of cards.

Jack stood back up, grabbed his wife's hand and took another glance at the Munger's front door. Then he raised his left arm and placed his hand on the doorframe. Bowing his head and closing his eyes, he prayed.

"Lord, please help this family in their time of need. We pray that thou will bless this family. Bestow thy grace upon them. The Munger's are a peaceful family. They are good people. We pray that their little girl will be found and returned home unscathed. Please watch over this family. Offer them comfort in their time of need. In Jesus' name, Amen."

Chapter 53

Jack and his wife turned and walked away from the house. They were nearly at the driveway when they heard a broken voice call out Jack's name.

The couple stopped and turned to see Julie standing in the doorway, tear stained face. They stood there, staring at each other, nobody saying a word. Then Jack broke the silence.

"We are so sorry for what your family is going through. We wanted to do something to help, so we made you dinner."

Jack motioned to the casserole dish on the chair.

Julie began to cry again, but it seemed as though her eyes were too dry to produce any more tears.

Through chokes and sobs, Julie tried to utter the words, "I,I,I, I'm s-s-s-s-so, s-s-sooor-ry. I,I, g-gave your n-n-naame t-t-to the p-p-police. I... I..."

"Julie, it's ok. I completely understand. I'm just worried about you and your girl. I just want to help any way I can."

Julie was hugging herself tightly around her mid-section. It looked like she was afraid that if she let go, her insides would drop to the ground. She was biting her lower lip, and her hair looked like she had developed a nervous habit of constantly running her hand through it.

"P-please, um-um, please, won't you come in?"

"Yes, of course, thank you."

Jack escorted his wife to the door, picked up the casserole and card, and followed after his wife into the house. As he passed Julie, she threw her arms around his neck and began sobbing. When she regained her composure, Jack handed her the card. She thanked him and took the casserole from his hands.

"Please, have a seat. I'll be with you in just a moment."

Chapter 54

The President was rushed through crowds of reporters and citizens who shouted questions and were demanding answers. The President hurried along with the forced smile on his face. He reached the portable staircase leading up to Air Force One.

He knew he was most vulnerable to attack during this climb. The Secret Service also knew this and stood on elevated alert each time the President made the traditional climb, pause, turn, and wave, before entering the safety of the plane. The Secret Service had argued for decades that this was the weak link in the security of the President. Proponents argued that the President was an elected official who must be seen by his constituents. The people loved to gather and witness this ascension and salutation. Many generations have witnessed the 'Man of the People' waving as he boarded the flying White House.

Roger Climmings, head of the Secret Service, stated that the President should be lifted to the plane within a steel, bulletproof shipping container and within the confines of a hanger and only at Air Force/Navy Bases. He also continually argued that it was only a matter of time before somebody gained just the right vantage point and took a shot at the President as he turned and waved. With the high-powered sniper rifles and all the men that have been trained by our own Armed Forces, it was only a matter of time.

These warnings went through the President's mind each and every time he climbed the staircase.

As he reached the top of the stairs, he looked for the "all clear" gesture from his security that stood just inside the plane. He was always poised to dive into the protective confines of the plane if there was any sign of worry on the face of the security waiting for him.

As he hurried up the stairs he watched their eyes as they scanned the crowds and surrounding areas. He continued to hold his breath as he saw a hand rise up. His heart stopped as his mind processed the distinction between a thumbs-up and a "hurry-stay-down-dive" gesture.

Seeing the rising hand transform into a thumbs-up, the President turned as he reached the top platform. With the forced smile and sweat dripping down his back, he raised his arm and waived to the people.

Just then a blinding reflection hit his face. He felt his body buckle over as he was yanked down and into the plane. The crowd erupted in gasps of confusion.

Nobody had heard any gunshots.

The live news coverage showed Secret Service members scanning the crowd and running around with one hand to an ear and the other poised ready to draw the weapon holstered to their sides.

Chapter 55

The President was given the all clear and was helped up off the floor of the plane.

He tried to never get upset with the men who protected him, but he often felt that he was more at risk of receiving injury as a result of their paranoia than anything else.

The men brushed him off and offered their apologies.

When the President asked for an explanation, the head of security informed him, "The men were blinded by what appeared to be press camera equipment reflecting the sun. They panicked and quickly reacted by pulling you into the safe confines of the plane."

The President understood and replied, "Well, better to be safe than sorry."

He then turned to his secretary and stated, "Please tell those waiting in the conference room that we will need to postpone the meeting by 30 minutes. I will need time to regain my composure and change into a clean suit."

She smiled and replied, "Yes, Sir, of course."

Chapter 56

Julie returned with her husband and a silver platter of ice waters.

"Jack, you remember my husband, Charles?"

Jack rose and shook his hand.

"Yes, we only met a few times while I was working on the place, but I remember. Good to see you. This is my wife, Tessy. Sorry, I failed to introduce her earlier. I had forgotten that you two had never met."

"Nice to finally meet you and to put a face to the name," Julie said as she shook Tessy's hand.

"Yes, I rarely have the opportunity to meet Jack's clients, but I do benefit from hearing all the stories. It is very nice to meet you both."

They all sat down, and there was an uncomfortable silence.

Jack began, "I'm sorry, but it has been a long time. For the life of me, I cannot remember either of your girls' names."

"Samantha and Sydney, and we have added a son since you were here last, his name is William," Julie informed.

"Oh, that's right. Gosh, it seems so long ago that I was here. You know, the toughest part of my job is getting close to the families of my clients, and then letting them go. It doesn't seem right. Many times I feel like part of the family."

"Yes, I can identify with that. We were sad to not have you coming around anymore. We grew accustomed to having you here. The girls really loved you." She choked on the words. "For weeks after you finished, they would ask when you were going to come back for a visit."

Jack nodded.

"Hey, where is your dog? He always greeted me at the door."

Julie looked at her glass of water. Charles fielded the question.

"Spanky is no longer with us. He apparently was attacked in our backyard by coyotes or a mountain lion."

"Oh My Gosh! Really? That's terrible," Tessy let out.

"Charles, you say this like you don't believe it," Jack inquired.

"Well, I'm no outdoorsman, tracker, or what-have-ya; but wild animals leave tracks. They also make a lot of noise when fighting a dog. And typically, these animals do not go after large animals like Spanky. He was a 96-pound Labradoodle. To add to the mystery, the gates were closed and there was not any damage to the fencing."

"So why did they think it was a wild animal?"

"I don't know. Probably because it looked like something had killed and eaten poor Spanky," Charles struggled to finish the sentence.

"How long ago did this happen?"

"About six months ago."

"That is so terrible. You guys have been dealing with some serious crap around here. I am so sorry.

"So about Samantha, do they have any leads? What is the status?"

"Search and Rescue is out combing the neighborhood, school, and the nearby open-space," Julie answered. "So far, there hasn't been any clues or news. It is as if she just vanished."

"Well, can they use more people to help search? We know a lot of people."

"No, we asked them, but they said that untrained searchers tend to overlook clues and destroy evidence. They have about 200 searchers out right now and they said that more would be coming this evening from other counties."

"So what do they want you to do, just sit here and twiddle your thumbs?"

"Well, they said that many times, missing children end up returning home on their own, or calling. So they wanted us to stay here encase she shows up."

"I guess that makes sense, but it has got to be aggravating for you both."

"I think it is more aggravating for Charles than me. He feels helpless. He wants to do something. Me, I can barely function, so I wouldn't be of much help out there. They'd probably be focused on me instead of trying to find my little girl."

"Well, we do not want to take anymore of your time. Like I said, we just wanted to bring you over some food and to let you know that you are in our prayers. Please, if you need anything, please, do not hesitate to call."

"Right, ok. Yes, well thank you both so much for stopping by and for the food. Again, I am so sorry to have dragged you into this. I really did not think you had done anything to hurt Sam, but they asked if anyone had ever shown an interest in her."

Julie looked completely torn apart.

"Julie, listen, you have enough on your plate to worry about without being concerned about my feelings. I completely understand and would have done the same thing if the roles were reversed. No hard feelings, honestly. The important thing is that they find your girl and bring her home. Let's focus on that."

They all exchanged hugs and made their way to the door.

"Really, thanks for stopping by and for being so understanding. We'll have to get together when all of this dies....(she paused)...when all of this blows over."

They all pretended not to notice Julie's careful correction of her choice of words.

"Yes, that would be lovely. I would love to get to know you better," Tessy followed.

Charles opened the front door as two officers approached the porch.

Chapter 57

The officers said their quick hellos and asked if they could have a moment. Jack and Tessy felt uncomfortable, but their curiosity kept them from voluntarily leaving.

"Yes, what is going on," Charles asked?

"We believe that we found your daughter, but there is terrible news. I'm awfully sorry," the officer stated.

Julie began to wail. She had enough. Her emotions had exhausted her. She fell against her husband and slowly collapsed to the floor. Tessy instinctually enveloped her within her arms and began rocking her back and forth.

Jack stood there stunned.

Charles was in shock. His eyes seemed to be looking at some distant horizon that only he could see.

Jack inquired, "are you absolutely sure that it is Samantha?"

"Yes, she is wearing the clothes as described."

"Clothes? Clothes? What about her face? Is it or is it not Samantha? Look at what you are doing to these poor people. You ought to be damn sure before presenting this terrible news."

Jack was not a confrontational man. He surprised himself at the way he was talking to the men in uniform. He felt compelled to defend the Mungers. He felt terrible for their loss and wanted desperately to help.

"Sir, I understand that this is stressful and upsetting. This isn't easy for any of us. Nobody likes to see children get hurt or families attacked. We are sure that the girl we found is Samantha. But, like with any investigation, we will confirm this with positive identification through dental records or fingerprinting."

"Was she raped," Charles managed to whisper.

"No sir, it does not appear that she was raped or suffered any form of sexual molestation. The attack does not appear to have been sexually motivated."

Charles focused his gaze on the officer as he processed what he had just said.

"Then what does appear to be the motivation for killing my daughter?"

Charles bit off each of his words as if he were accusing the officer himself of killing his daughter.

"Sir, I'm sorry for your loss, I really am. If you'd like I can have a chaplain come and visit with you."

"Don't patronize me. You are telling me that my daughter was murdered and I'd like to know why."

"I really do not think that you would want to hear this. I don't see how…"

"I'M NOT INTERESTED IN WHAT YOU THINK! ALL I WANT TO KNOW IS WHY MY DAUGHTER IS DEAD! EITHER YOU TELL ME OR PUT ME IN TOUCH WITH SOMEONE WHO CAN!"

"Sir, I'm not the bad guy here, I'm just the messenger."

As Charles attempted to regain his composure, Tessy lifted her head.

She addressed the officer, "We know that your intentions are good. We realize that you are trying to spare the Mungers, but please. They want to know."

"Ok, well… Um," the officer cleared his throat. "It appears as though a wild animal attacked Samantha. Her remains were found less than a mile from here, in the open space."

Julie looked up with tear soaked cheeks. "Where is she? I want to see my girl. Can you take me to her?"

"Well, I really do not think that would be good for anyone."

"Why not? I want to see her."

The officer shook his head.

Jack interjected, "why do you think that it wouldn't be a good idea?"

"I do not want to upset you more than I already have."

"Go ahead officer, please tell us," Charles urged.

"Listen, we were not able to identify her by her face. Do you understand what I am saying? No parent should see his or her child like that, it is not healthy. Nothing good could come of that. Nothing."

They waited for the officers to leave, and then Julie turned to her husband for answers. She expected him to make everything better. She wanted him to fix this. He fixed everything. She wanted this fixed.

"First Spanky and now Samantha? What is going on here? What kind of animal are we dealing with," Julie asked.

"I do not know, but I think it is high past time that we organize a hunting party," answered Charles.

"I have never hunted before, but I have guns, and you can count me in," Jack offered.

"Great, let's call a few guys and we head out tonight."

"Sounds good to me. We're going to head home and get ready. Shall we say 9:00?"

"Actually, I was thinking a bit earlier than that. Animals tend to hunt right at dusk, let's head out about 6 or 6:30."

"Ok, you got it. I'll be back."

Chapter 58

The only place that Blythe felt at ease anymore was in her lab. She placed her iPod in the dock mounted on the wall next to the light switch. She selected a playlist, "Serotonin," and pushed play. The playlist consisted of a number of her favorites from the 80's. The quiet room sprang to life with the sound of Bizarre Love Triangle by New Order. She spun her finger around the circular control of her iPod, sending the volume up as high as it would go. She successfully drowned out the world with the music and her task at hand.

She told the Sheriff that she would look at the animals, but she didn't say when.
She pulled a gurney from the fridge, yanked off the blue-green paper hospital covering, and positioned the large operating lamp overhead. She stared in wonder, as she looked awkwardly at the numerous bite marks on the victim's body. She shook her head as if forcing herself out of a cloud. She reached over with her gloved hand and pushed record on her computer monitor.

The computer was connected to a video recorder as well as an audio recorder. Dr. Aspen began speaking as she examined the corpse.

"Adult male, appears to be in his fifties, covered in various bite marks. Some marks appear to be canine while others are definitely human. Scratch marks on body and thighs, maybe defensive wounds, could be offensive as well."

She picked up one of the man's hands, "Nails are blood stained, but do not show signs of defense."

She looked closely at the bites, "canine bites occurred postmortem suggesting animals were acting instinctually as scavengers, as opposed to violently attacking the victim. The canines may have been coyotes…" Blythe trailed off in thought.

Coyotes, she thought of the dead pets yet to be examined. Could they be connected? Are coyotes killing more than pets? She turned back to the task at hand, cognizant that the recorders were running.

She looked closely at the human bite marks.

"Victim sustained significant trauma as a result of human bites. The human bites appear to have been sustained before the death of the victim."

Blythe reached over to the computer screen and pushed pause on the recording devices. She took another look at the body and then rushed out of the examination room.

Pushing her body into the door of Lab 3, Blythe went straight for the walk-in fridge. She quickly located the remains of the animals. She shook her head as she counted 6 corpses.

The Sheriff is pushy, if nothing else.

She touched the overhead light and pulled it down over the corpses. The light sprung to life with a hum. The entire gurney was flooded with light. Blythe then understood the Sheriff's urgency.

There, before her, she was looking at partially eaten remains of pets; four dogs and two cats. They appeared to be torn apart, but there were obvious signs of human bite marks. The bite marks would have been obvious to an untrained person.

Blythe selected an electric shaver from the tray of tools. She turned it on and began shaving what was left of the abdomen of one of the cats.

As the fur fell to the gurney, she looked in astonishment. She quickly began shaving one of the dogs, and then she moved on to the other animals. On all six of the animals, she found the same thing, the cause of death for these animals and the human she had been examining were all the same, eaten alive... by humans.

Chapter 59

Sheriff Glasgow had been anxiously awaiting the phone call from Dr. Aspen. He highly respected her expertise and often bragged that she was the best in the business and that he had found her.

Truth be told, he had watched her grow up and always felt like a pseudo-father figure. She may not remember, but he had given her, her first chemistry set. He saw potential in her that nobody else had. She immediately had a love for science and he pushed her to excel.

He imagined she would be a surgeon or a medical doctor. But Blythe decided that she wanted to help solve crimes; a product of Hollywood sensationalizing crime scene investigating. David tried to steer her into a more glamorous field, but she insisted. It worked out well enough; he was able to land her a job and kept her close to home. Besides, he capitalized on her expertise and position more than a few times.

The Sheriff refused to leave his desk until the call came in. Sheriff Glasgow saw the animal corpses first hand. He insisted on looking at them when his deputy reported seeing human bite marks.

Deputy Blayne Stevens was a great employee. He worked hard and long hours and never complained. He didn't even complain when he was demoted from a patrol officer to animal control. The Sheriff made this move for him; it was either that or losing his job altogether. He wasn't cut out for the force.

He was a man with lots of ambition. His Dad was a cop and he wanted to be just like him. Problem was that he wasn't strong and he lacked street smarts. He was intelligent enough to pass the entire test with flying colors, but a cop who wasn't streetwise, ended up dead.

When Deputy Stevens reported human bite marks on several animals, he didn't question him, but at the same time he did not altogether believe him.

Chapter 60

The President stood just before the door of his private entrance into the conference room aboard Air Force One. He knew that the members on the other side awaited an explanation for his unusual press release. He drew a deep breath, let it out slow, and then grasped and turned the doorknob.

When he walked in, the room was alive with conversation. Most of the members were standing. Within several seconds, a respectful quite engulfed the room. Automatically, without invitation, everyone moved to stand by their assigned chairs that surrounded the conference table.

The President took his chair and requested, "Please, be seated."

He began, "Many of you know what is going on, some of you know more than I do, and the rest need to be informed. So we are here so that we can all be caught up to speed and so that we can be on the same page.

"The press conference at the CDC where I was administered the Influenza Vaccine was a last minute emergency to address a possible epidemic. I am neither a doctor nor a scientist, so I will turn this portion of our discussion over to Dr. Shu-Medly from the CDC in Atlanta. Dr. Shu-Medly."

"Yes, thank you Mr. President." Dr. Shu-Medly began as he stood up. "To catch each of you up to speed, the CDC in Atlanta has a division called the Bio-Terror Division. This division was set up to find cures, antibodies, vaccines, etc. for possible Bio-terrorist attacks. Part of this task involves predicting what the enemy may develop. In order to develop a response to a biological attack, we must first develop and understand the attack.

"For example, if the enemy were to release a strand of influenza, we must have that strand before we can develop a vaccine that would combat the spread of the virus. This is primarily how we predict and prepare for the flu season each year. This year, however, brought about an unforeseen problem.

"About a decade ago, a group at the CDC began to wonder if the rise in interest about Zombies, might create an effort to develop a biological weapon that would cause us to kill and eat ourselves. A small group began working on the development of such a weapon with the intention of developing a cure."

A few of the men began to murmur and whisper to each other. Dr. Shu-Medly heard one close to him whisper under his breath, "Sounds like the makings of a Marvel Comic."

"Please, please, try and stay with me," Dr. Shu-Medly pleaded with his hands raised. "I have a lot to tell you about, so please pay attention so we can cover this and answer questions during this flight."

The doctor continued, "The scientist developed a sort of bacteria that creates an urge within the infected to feed on meat. The bacterium was appropriately named: Carnivorous Bacterialus. I admit that it sounds absurd, it sounds like a bad sci-fi horror movie, but I assure you that it is true. Some of you may recall crazy stories in our recent past of people who have been attacked and had their faces bitten. It is now believed that these cases may have some correlation and was not merely random acts of peculiar violence.

"The first reported case occurred in Gainesville, GA, not too far removed from the Atlanta CDC. In fact, many of the employees of the CDC reside and commute from this area."

"Now, how could this get out of the controlled environment of the CDC," the Doctor asked rhetorically.

"Unfortunately, we discovered sometime ago, that the air circulation of the CDC labs were cross contaminating the air. The contained labs were originally designed to be self-contained and completely separated from the other locations of the lab. This turned out, not to be the case. A portion of the air ducts were somehow connected at one point and the small amount of the contaminated air bypassed the filtration system. The result being that the contaminated air exposed the unprotected employees to unknown contaminants. This has been the case since the lab opened.

"We finally realized the problem when a majority of our staff fell ill last week with a strain of influenza that the lab had developed. Inadvertently, this created strain was released into the public realm. The good news is that we have the vaccine, for which you all saw the President receiving this morning. The bad news is that we cannot be sure that the strain has not mutated beyond the effectiveness of the vaccine.

"Furthermore, with recent reports of an unprecedented demand for meat products, we fear that the influenza strain may have combined in the air ducts with the Carnivorous Bacterialus.

"Based on this theory, we are urging everyone to receive the influenza vaccine, and we hope that this will prevent the spread and potential epidemic of this bacteria."

Chapter 61

It was now day three since Malcolm had checked in with the Spot device. Brenda was extremely worried. She dialed the number for the Summit Ranger Station in Pinecrest.

After making it through the call tree of weather reports, fire restrictions, and permit information; she finally got through to a live person.

"Summit Ranger Station, how can I help you?"

"Hello, my name is Brenda Jenkins. My husband is currently backpacking in the Emigrant Wilderness. He has a Spot locator on him that he has been checking in on daily. I have not heard from him in three days now, and I fear that he may need help."

"Ok, ma'am. I'll need to get some information from you. What is your husband's name?"

"Malcolm, Malcolm Jenkins."

"Great, please hold while I look to see if he pulled a permit. I have to make sure that he entered the wilderness."

Brenda was upset that she was put on hold. She didn't want this guy thinking that she was just a worried wife. She wondered how she could convey to him the severity of the situation.

"Ok, Ma'am, I've got his permit here. He's scheduled to exit today. He put that he was heading to Woods Lake. Is that what he told you?"

"Yes. His last report from the Spot was just East of Woods Lake, that was three days ago."

"Ok, it also states that he was alone, is that correct?"

"Yes."

"Alright, can you give me a description of your husband?"

"Yes, of course. Um, he is white with brown wavy hair. He's 5'10" and weighs 175 pounds. Um, what else can I tell you?"

"Uh, yea, well unfortunately, you just described every man in the wilderness. Can you tell me what he might be wearing, the color of his backpack, a description of his tent, anything that would set him apart from the other hikers?"

"Oh, I don't know. Let me think. I don't know what his tent looks like; I don't ever go with him. Oh, I know that his backpack is red and he wears this ugly worn brownish ranger looking hat. You know, a Fedora like Indiana Jones wears?"

"Perfect, that will help a lot. Did you say that he had a Spot Satellite GPS Messenger?"

"Yes, he does, but he hasn't responded in three days."

"Ok, do you happen to have the serial number and 8 digit code for his unit?"

"Um. Let me see. No, not right here, but I can look it up."

"Great, if you can get that to me, then we can try and locate him, as long as it is on, of course. Ok, I'm going to contact my Ranger in the field and ask him to hike over to your husband's LKP."

"LKP?"

"Last Known Point. I'm also going to notify a group of packers, heading out with mules today, to keep an eye out for him. And I'll send a ranger over to check to see if his vehicle is still at the trailhead. As soon as I hear anything, I'll get in touch with you. Is this the number to call you back on?"

"Yes, this is my mobile, I'll keep this on me."

"OK, great. I wouldn't worry too much; the batteries always die in those things and people often spend an extra day out there. We'll look into it and let you know what we find."

"Great, thanks-so-much. And what was your name?"

"Tom Watkins."

"Ok, thanks Tom, I really appreciate this."

"No problem ma'am, that's what we are here for."

Chapter 62

The Sheriff sat at his desk, remembering how the nightmare began.

Deputy Stevens pulled the animal control truck into the driveway and waited as the automatic chain linked gate rolled to the side. Sheriff Glasgow was already standing in the parking lot awaiting his arrival.

Blayne pulled up and turned off the engine. He leaped down from the cab and shook hands with his boss.

"You are not going to believe this," Blayne said as he began opening one of the six cages on the driver's side of the vehicle.

The Sheriff peaked inside the cage at the carcass of a dog. The canine appeared to be torn apart as if something had been eating it.

"Stevens, you reported seeing human bite marks," the Sheriff inquired.

"Yes, I did. The strangest thing, I didn't notice them at first. But after picking up the fifth carcass, I saw the pattern. Then I checked the others, sure enough, they all have human bite marks. Check this out," she said as she gloved her hand and yanked the dog out onto the ground.

The large German Shepherd was stiff and plunked to the ground like a sack of wheat falling from the truck. Deputy Stevens brushed back the fur that was stiffened with dried blood. The smell of a rotting corpse was never appealing, but you got use to it.

The Sheriff squatted next to the corpse on display. He removed his sunglasses and examined the remains, trying to make sense of what he was seeing. He caulked his head and peered into Blayne's eyes. He returned his gaze with a look that seemed to say, *Told you they were human bite marks.*

"Stevens, how many of these animals do you reckon you've picked up with similar markings?"

"Well Sheriff, I don't really know. What I do know is that today was the first time I realized that the bites were human. But I have seen a surge in the number of dead animals that have been gnawed on over the passed few months. But six of them in one morning has to be the record."

"Ok, we may have a problem here. I am going to have Dr. Aspen take a look at these. I want you to call your department and put a hold on the cremations of any corpses that still remain."

"Will do, Sir."

Chapter 63

Dr. Aspen pulled off her gloves and gown and quickly made her way down the hall toward her office. She passed by Lab 3 where her playlist was currently playing, "It's a Dead Man's Party" by Oingo Boingo.

"Well, Danny Elfman, you got that right," she said aloud to herself.

She burst into her office, grabbed her desk phone, and began dialing as she dropped into her chair.

"Blythe, speak to me, what did you find?" The Sheriff shouted into the receiver.

Blythe hadn't even heard the phone ring, he sounded extremely anxious – understandable under the circumstances.

"Sheriff, it appears that the animals suffered and died from being eaten alive. But the strange thing is that it appears that the bite marks are human."

The Sheriff interrupted, "Yes, that was my findings as well. I wanted you to confirm that. We may have a person out there hunting people's pets. But you think they were alive?"

"Yes, some of the human bite marks were sustained before the animals expired. There are canine bite marks, but they occurred post-mortem," Blythe confirmed.

"So we have a deranged guy out there, snatching pets, and chewing on them until they die? Why would he not hide his handy work or finish consuming the animals?"

"Sheriff, that is your expertise, not mine. Maybe he get's his fill and moves on. Maybe he gets scared off. Maybe he is just out for the kill. Maybe he wants to be caught."

"Well, whomever he is, he's extremely active. It appears that he has been at this for sometime and is stepping up his game. Those six pets were just from this morning. I've got an office full of people asking about missing pets and wondering what is going on. I don't think they are going to buy into the Mountain Lion story any longer. Well, thanks for looking into this for me. I know this is unprecedented and outside of your call of duty, thanks for helping. I've got to figure out what to do with this information."

"Sheriff, there is more," Blythe interrupted.

The Sheriff did not like the sound in Dr. Aspen's voice. He knew by her tone, that what she was about to share would be worse than what she had already told him.

"Aspen, what is it?" He prodded.

"I have a body here that I'm performing an autopsy on. Male in his fifties, with bite marks." She paused to allow this to settle-in. "I don't know for sure what we are looking at, I still have to perform the autopsy, but I wanted to let you know sooner rather than later."

"Shit, we may have a psychopath that has escalated from animals to humans. This puts another dimension to this bizarre case."

"Sheriff, I was thinking that we should have somebody take impressions from these bite marks on all the animals and the human. They should be compared to make sure that we are talking about one perp here," Blythe advised.

The Sheriff was impressed at the level-headedness of Dr. Aspen. This was one of the main reasons he liked her so much. She was professional and always on top of her game.

"You are right," he said. "I will send a crime scene investigator right away. I am going to contact the FBI as well. There's a chance that this guy is killing outside of my jurisdiction and I definitely would like their expertise on this one. Especially a profiler, so we know what to look for."

Chapter 64

Pamela had responded as soon as Brenda called her. She had picked her up from her place in less than an hour from the time she received the call. They now were heading east on CA-120 toward the Sierras.

Brenda received a call from the ranger. They found Malcolm's vehicle, could not locate his Spot, and by the end of the day, neither the field Ranger or Packers had spotted him.

In no condition mentally to drive, Brenda called her girlfriend to accompany her on the journey. Pamela did not even hesitate; she grabbed her jump bag, threw in some extra clothes and snacks, and was out the door in 15 minutes flat.

Now they sat in a line of traffic heading through Manteca. Brenda had been taking calls throughout their drive.

"Ok, thanks. Yes, we are on our way, about 2 hours or so to go. Alright, we'll see you then. Bye."

"What's going on now," Pamela asked.

"They have a search organized, some heading out today and the rest to begin in the morning. They currently have a couple of rangers in the field and a few pack teams are keeping their eyes open. They also have somebody at the trailheads to interview everyone as they come out. They said to drive straight to the Pinecrest Community Center, we can stay the night there. He said that they are organizing from there."

Brenda's voice was shaking.

"He is in his element. It is a good thing that they haven't found anything yet. That means that he isn't hurt on the trail. He's probably off having fun and forgot what day it was. He's going to be fine."

Brenda just nodded her head. She turned to gaze out the window at the passing orchards of almond trees. She bit her nails as her eyes danced along the swooshing rows of trees.

The women drove in mostly silence from that point on.

Chapter 65

Unable to proceed with the autopsy and awaiting investigators, Dr. Aspen went to the break room to see if anything decent remained in the fridge. She pulled open the large stainless steel door. There were numerous bags and small boxes of leftover takeout from various restaurants. She grabbed the first brown bag.

Though no name was present, she recognized the bag as being from the Taqueria down the street. Maybe there was half a super burrito or at least some tortilla chips to snack on. Since her lunch hour was cut short, she was starving.

She opened the bag and nearly dropped it in disgust. The whole interior of the bag was covered in mold.

She wondered how long this had been in there, but really did not want to know.

She could handle dead bodies, the stench of a body in decay, but when it came to rotting moldy food, she had a hard time holding her cookies.

Dr. Aspen tossed the bag into the trash and opted for a can of Coke. She drank the coke as she roamed down the hallway of the now vacant building. Most of the people she worked with clocked in around 9:30am and left their office by 3:00pm.

This kind of waste was why she always voted no for any kind of tax increase. Her opinion was the public agencies received too much funding, but that they were like spoiled rich kids who would always cry for more. She wanted to see a reduction in taxes and force agencies to reduce waste.

She looked out the back window into the dirt overflow parking lot. It was full with county vehicles that for the most part sat unused. The county purchased new vehicles every year, but regulation prevented them from disposing of the used vehicles until they reached 80,000 miles. Nobody wanted to drive an older vehicle when a nice shiny new one was available. So the vehicles were 'put out to pasture' in the back lot. She shook her head and kept walking to the front door.

Blythe stood outside, leaning against the handicap handrail that ran along the concrete ramp. She waited there for her guest and finished sipping on her Coke. She began thinking about all the things she could be working on, instead of standing idle. Her mind went to the 12 bodies waiting for autopsy.

She couldn't get started on an autopsy; she knew she would be interrupted and have to let the investigators into the building. She cursed under her breath that Trish had to leave to go get her dang fleabag.

As she thought about her impending task, she began to wonder about the possibility of the other 11 bodies having suffered a similar demise. With that thought, she yanked at her key card, stressing the capability of the retractable cord, waved it over the black square reader, and impatiently yanked open the door.

Chapter 66

Dr. Aspen tossed the empty can into the trash in the lobby. She never bothered with separating for recycling. She figured the routine performed by millions was simply free labor for the trash collecting companies.

They collected the pre-sorted trash, bundled, and then turned it in for redemption. Not only were they benefiting from free labor and redemption values; they were also charging for the collection of the waste. What a scam. She was disgusted with how ignorant and gullible people could be.

She intentionally used her recycling bin as her primary trash receptacle and 'stuck it to the man' by only paying for the smallest available trash container. These small acts of rebellion always put a smile on her face.

She rushed into Lab 1 and barely took time to put on the gown and gloves. She rushed over to the pull out drawers that contained the bodies. They only had six of these drawers, the rest of the bodies were waiting in the walk-in fridge of Labs 2 & 3.

She yanked open the first drawer and pulled back the covering, exposing the naked remains. She quickly looked over the body. The abdomen was gnawed and missing.

She opened the next drawer, yanked the sheet, allowing it to pillow on the floor behind her. She looked down at a teenaged girl who had bloody holes where her breast should be and was missing her face.

Blythe found herself tearing up but continued. She yanked open the third drawer. The woman was missing fingers, chunks of flesh had been removed from various portions of her body. Her ears and nose were missing. Her skin was stained red.

Next Blythe went into autopilot and hastily yanked open the remaining drawers and exposed the remaining bodies. All of them had been feasted upon.

Feeling like she was in a horror-flick, Dr. Aspen stumbled out of the room. Her tear-filled eyes were blurring her vision as she stumbled backward into the hall. She braced herself against the wall facing the door from whence she had exited. She noticed that she was hyperventilating.

Chapter 67

The women pulled into the Pinecrest Community Center. There was a helicopter in the parking lot and several rescue vehicles. A few people congregated around the large boulders in front of the brown building.

The women approached the building. One of the guys stood up and asked if he could assist them.

He was tall and slender, his hair hung in long dreadlocks that bounced as he moved his head. His skin browned from a summer of sun. His hands were stained with dirt, undoubtedly a climber. Like the others with him, he wore a yellow t-shirt that displayed that he was part of Yosemite Search and Rescue.

"I'm Brenda Jenkins, I was told to come here."

"OH! Yes, hello. My name is Makunda. I'm with Yosemite Search and Rescue, we're just waiting for our assignment and then we'll be heading out. Conditions are excellent, so we are planning to hike through the night."

"Oh, thank you guys so much. I know that it is dangerous to hike at night, so thank you."

"No, no problem. We are looking forward to it. There's a full moon and clear skies, we won't even need flashlights tonight. Don't you worry, I'm sure your husband is fine. We'll find him for you. We all know these woods extremely well. If he wants to be found, we'll find him."

Brenda thought this was a strange comment, but she nodded anyway. Pamela put her arm around her shoulders and ushered her up the deck boards and into the building.

Inside, the place was busy. There were maps on walls and across tables. Flyers with Malcolm's picture and description were posted on every wall. People were discussing plans. Highlighters were rolling off tables and radios cackled. A man in uniform stood in the middle of the room, clearly in charge, and observing his subordinates.

He yelled, "PLANS! HURRY UP! I'VE GOT A TEAM – SITTING OUTSIDE - READY TO GO. DAYLIGHT IS BURNING, WHERE'S THEIR ASSIGNMENT?"

A voice called out from a woman hunched over and writing feverously, "Almost finished. MAPS. I need maps!"

"Right here," another woman yelled out as she slammed the maps on the table.

"Is the assignment highlighted? Can somebody read this to make sure it makes sense?"

"THERE'S NO TIME, JUST PUT IT TOGETHER SO THE TEAM CAN BE BRIEFED AND RELEASED! THEY'LL FIGURE IT OUT IN TRANSIT. LET'S GO! LET'S GO! MOVE IT!" The uniformed man was yelling out.

The room began frantically passing the packet along. Each time the packet was given to a new person, the packet grew. Maps, instructions, protocols, flyers. Finally, an older gentleman grabbed the packet and ran outside.

It was then that the Ranger noticed the women standing at the door. He smiled and moved toward them.

"MRS. JENKINS? WELCOME! WELCOME!" He yelled loudly, probably to notify the room of their presence.

"Please, come in. I'm Tom, we spoke on the phone. This is all for your husband. We have several teams in the field already. Then we'll release this last team and then it's just a waiting game until the morning. We are currently just using local search and rescue, which includes the team from the ski resort and Yosemite. We have teams responding in the morning from neighboring counties. This isn't much, but we'll be here all night. There's a back room where people will be sleeping, you're welcome to crash there. I'm sorry that we do not have better accommodations for you."

"No, that's fine. I really do not think that I'll be getting much sleep tonight."

"Right. I suspect that to be true."

Chapter 68

Consciously she slowed her heartbeat and regained her composure. She really wished that others were around. Usually she enjoyed the peace and quiet of the evenings when everyone left early. Her most productive time of day was the evening when she could work without interruptions.

Though she didn't want to, she knew she had to check the remaining corpses. She slowly walked to the door of Lab 2. She slowly reached out her hand for the door handle. She couldn't help but think that this is the part in the movie where something startling happens to the poor girl who is alone.

She paused with her hand on the handle, willing herself to enter. She took a deep breath and pushed down on the knob as she put her weight into the door.

Just at that moment she heard loud banging, a loud buzzer, and her phone began to vibrate. She jumped out of her skin and she waited for her heart to begin pumping again.

When the blood returned to her face, she hurried toward the front door while pulling out her phone.

"Aspen."

The Sheriff chimed, "my guys are there waiting at the front door, where are you?"

"Yes, I hear them, I'm letting them in now. Sheriff, we have a serious mess on our hands, you may want to come down and see this first handed."

"I can not get away, the office is a zoo right now. I've got reporters setting up camp and wanting a statement. I have to figure out what to tell them. Just tell me what you are looking at," the Sheriff replied impatiently.

"David, all of the bodies down here have been chewed on."

The banging and the buzzing continued. The team outside could not see through the tinted glass that Blythe was standing there talking on the phone.

"What? This is turning into a freaking horror movie."

"Funny, I was thinking the same thing," Blythe replied.

"I can not imagine that this is the works of one man. We maybe looking at a cult, gone haywire. Maybe these are rituals?"

"I don't know, but I am officially freaked out. I'm considering camping out here where it is safe, until this all blows over."

"Not a bad idea. You will be tied up there for sometime anyway, my guys are waiting to take impressions, and hopefully I can get Feebie to get down there this evening."

"I would think that the Feds would be all over this. I haven't been able to get ahold of anyone to tell them the severity of it all. This thing just keeps growing and so far I've only been talking to voicemails."

"Hey, your guys are getting impatient. I'll call you back," Blythe ended the call without waiting for a return farewell.

Chapter 69

Dr. Shu-Medley now had the full-attention of everyone who was privileged enough - and met the security clearances – to be present in the meeting aboard Air Force One. He loved having the spotlight. Today, at this very moment, the Doctor finally felt that he was earning the respect and command that his superior knowledge deserved. He was talking slowly, not only so the inferiors could understand, but to lavish in the moment.

"Now, we know that this causes an urge to consume meat, but scientist have not observed this translating into cannibalism. So far, they have witnessed omnivores preferring ground beef to their customary plant-based diets. But there is reason to believe that if the meat is not available, the infected may adapt and move on to more drastic measures to satisfying their cravings."

The doctor then walked around the table and flicked on a wide screen monitor mounted high on the wall. A map of the United States appeared on the screen with lights appearing indicating major cities.

The doctor explained, "Each of these lights depicts major airports around our country. Perhaps most of you are familiar with how quickly disease spreads. If we assume the worse, this Carnivorous Bacterialus induced influenza beginning in Atlanta, quickly spreads with the flights departing out of Hartsfield-Jackson Atlanta International Airport."

Dr. Shu-Medly pushed the button on the small remote he held in his hand. They watched in amusement, shock, and fear as the monitor sprung to life. Lighted pathways indicated the spread of the influenza along the flight paths. Soon the map morphed into the globe and depicted the spread worldwide. A clock on the bottom right corner of the screen ticked along showing that within 24 hours, the disease could potentially reach all around the world.

Dr. Shu-Medly broke the trance, "Please realize that this is only demonstrating the spread of influenza via air travel. We must also remain aware that it will travel by road, rail, and waterways. It can also spread with winds. What we do not know at this point, is if the disease can spread from human to animal and vice versa."

"Oh great, we have an avian flu on steroids created by our own government!" the Secretary of State interjected.

The room erupted in debate. Dr. Shu-Medly failed to regain order.

Chapter 70

Blythe opened the door and held it open while the team came in, all carrying briefcases and equipment.

"Come in, come in. I'm Dr. Aspen, I know some of your faces. Hope you guys didn't just eat. Please, come in."

"Dr. Aspen, I'm Don Spincalli. We met at the last staff appreciation gala. I'll be heading up this portion of the investigation. The Sheriff said that there were bite impressions that we should gather off of a body and some animals?"

"Yes, only it has now grown to several corpses. Here, follow me."

Don walked behind her and asked, "several animal corpses or several bodies?"

He asked as he stared down. He noticed that she was in great shape and her dress hugged her rear rump revealing a perfectly rounded shape before falling straight against the back of her moving legs. Her calf muscles were accentuated by the angle caused by the high-heels she wore on her feet. Don could recognize and admire beauty in the worst of situations.

"Yes," was Dr. Aspens shortened response.

Don had to remind himself of the question he had asked. "Wait, several animal... and... human corpses? What is going on here?"

"You'll see, let's start in Lab 1." Blythe announced as if she were a realtor offering a tour in a mansion.

She opened the door to the lab and let the crew enter. It seemed that they all gasped in unison.

There, before them, laid six drawers pulled open with exposed naked bodies of various stages of consumption.

Chapter 71

Ranger Tom Deaver gave Brenda and Pamela a quick tour around the CP (Command Post). They could hear the sound of the pilot turning on the engines to the helicopter.

"It is going to be a bit noisy for a little while here."

Brenda nodded and then watched out the window as the propellers began spinning, picking up speed. She saw the pilot speaking into his headset, and instantly heard his voice on the radios.

The pilot revved up the engines to high piercing volume. It sounded as if the whole thing would fall apart at any moment. Then he waved his arm and instantly a group of men ran toward the helicopter. They were all hunched over, wearing helmets and carrying their backpacks like babes in their arms.

One by one, the men tossed in their packs and climbed aboard.

The helicopter was military; a large Blackhawk, painted forest green.

Each one of the guys inside the machine had grins from ear to ear. Two of the guys began snapping pictures of each other.

Boys will always be boys, Brenda thought to herself.

Brenda and Pamela both thought that the noise of the helicopter could not possibly get any louder, but then the noise climbed exponentially. Most of the people present covered their ears. Then the helicopter raised a couple of inches and bobbled in the air. Then it balanced out, and the machine lifted straight up into the sky.

The thumping sound could be heard for several minutes as the helicopter flew east into the mountains.

Tom was the first to speak, "that is the most dangerous part of any search, but believe me, the guys love it."

"Yeah, it looks exhilarating; they all looked extremely delighted."

"Yes, sorry about that. These guys live and breath this stuff. They are highly trained and are like dogs chasing a stick. They get so excited to put their skills to the test. Truly they do not mean any disrespect."

"No, No. I understand. I'm just glad that they are out there helping."

"Sir, we truly appreciate all everyone is doing here," Pamela attempted to interject.

"Right. Well, again, I apologize. Please bear in mind that most of the people that you will see here are volunteers. They are foregoing work, vacations, families, and what have you. They respond for a number of reasons, mainly just to help and serve their fellow men."

"We understand and are deeply grateful," Pamela stated while glancing at Brenda.

"Yes, we are truly grateful," Brenda followed Pamela's lead.

Chapter 72

"Don, where would you like to start?" Dr. Aspen inquired.

Don had forgotten all about checking out Dr. Aspen's figure. He stood there, taking in the messy bodies. He had seen his share of gruesome crime scenes in his short 8-year career. He had seen more than a few multiple homicide crime scenes, but he had never witnessed this kind of gruesomeness.

Not receiving a response, Dr. Aspen offered, "Perhaps you should see the rest and then decide where to begin?"

Don nodded, apparently unable to utter a response.

They made their way passed Lab 2 and straight to Lab 3.

"I haven't looked at the bodies in Lab 2, I was just about to when I heard you banging at the front door."

"Oh, yes. Sorry about that, we were out there for a while and figured you couldn't hear us. We radioed in for the Sheriff to call you." Don finally spoke.

"Yes, I got his call. In here is where the pets are," She continued with the tour.

As she opened the door, it was apparent that her music was still playing. She had forgotten that she left it going. The tune of "No One Lives Forever" by Oingo Boingo was in mid-chorus. Her face turned beet-red as she reached for the pause button.

Don looked at her with one eyebrow lifted. His expression conferring the statement, "Really?"

Dr. Aspen led the team around the lab to show them the dead animal corpses. She continued to act as a guide, sharing with them how she shaved the bodies to expose the bite marks. They all shook their heads, as if agreeing with her tactics. It was surreal and strange to have an investigations team in her lab. Except for the occasional intern or curious citizen, she was usually in these labs alone.

Don spoke next, "Well let's have a look and see what we find in Lab 2. After you," he stated with an invitational outstretched arm.

"Right this way," Dr. Aspen said as she led the way to Lab 2.

Chapter 73

Lab 2 was an identical floor plan of Lab 3. There was a large examination room with a walk-in fridge on the far wall. The room was empty. They made their way to the fridge.

Dr. Aspen reached for the pull handle on the large door. She was cognizant of how much better she felt, now that others were with her.

She yanked on the door and stood to the side. The team entered the fridge. As Blythe entered the cold room, the door closed behind her. The slam of the door behind her made several of the guys jump. Blythe contained her grin.

The breeze created from the closing of the door made the sheets slightly move, emanating an eerie appearance that the corpses were moving. Even after the sheets stopped moving, it still looked like the chest were rising and falling.

Blythe remembered being a little girl at a viewing. She swore that her Great Grandmother was breathing in her casket. She told her father that it looked like GiGi was breathing.

Her father explained that it always looked like dead people were breathing because as humans we are so accustomed to seeing the chest rise and fall.

This didn't make sense to Blythe at the time, but in her graduate studies, she learned all about the phenomenon. Now as she stared at the bodies, she could not remember the name of the phenomenon.

She wondered if it bothered the other guys.

One of Don's partners chimed in, "I keep expecting one of these guys to rise up and start attacking us."

"It is starting to feel like the beginning of a George Romero film," Don conferred.

Blythe shook her head as if to shun the men for behaving like teenaged boys, even though she was feeling similarly.

She advanced to the nearest gurney and slowly pulled back the sheet.

The team moved in for a closer look. This body was a woman in her mid-twenties. There were no signs of trauma. They searched over the body for bite marks but did not find any.

"Obviously she died of other causes," Blythe concluded.

She covered the body back up.

"Or the perp was scared off before he could strap on his napkin," Don added.

Blythe uncovered the next body, revealing several cuts, bruises, and bite marks, but no missing flesh.

"This is growing stranger by the minute," Don offered.

Blythe uncovered the next body to reveal a corpse that was missing half a body. All of them jumped several feet back. Don knocked over a tray of instruments.

Blythe rolled her eyes as she moved on. Each of the following bodies had various degrees of missing parts. They stood there in silence trying to make sense of the nightmare they seemed to be trapped in.

Don spoke first, "Ok, Charlie, you take Lab 1. Brian, you get the mutts in Lab 3. I'll stay in here. First thing the Sheriff needs to know is if we are dealing with one guy or many. So let's get impressions made and pictures to document the bite marks. None of us wants to be here all night, so let's get moving. Also, Feebies can arrive at any moment, let's be ready to impress them, eh? Alright, go."

The team dispersed as if they were Navy Seals on the battlefield.

Boys will be Boys, Blythe thought to herself.

Chapter 74

After a week of searching, Ranger Tom called the searching off.
Search teams from all over California had responded. Brenda and
Pamela had seen teams from San Bernadino, Contra Costa,
Marin, Solano, and Yosemite. For the past week, there were 200
to 300 searchers in the woods looking for her husband. Nothing
was ever found, not a shoe, compass, or water bottle belonging to
Malcolm.

Brenda was distraught. Several clues came in, but none of them
were Malcolm's. She was both excited and nervous when a hiking
boot was found. But it turned out to be too big to be Malcolm's.

Brenda broke down in tears and sobbed for several minutes when
Ranger Tom told her that they had to suspend the search. A
week had passed, hundreds of searchers had been dispatched,
and tens of thousands of dollars had been spent. She understood
the reasoning, but she just could not stop the tears from falling.

What had happened to Malcolm? She wondered if he had been
eaten by a Bear, fallen off a cliff, or drowned?

The weeks leading up to his trip, he had been acting so aloof. His midnight runs had become longer. His jacket had blood on it. He began to distance himself from her. She felt it. She wondered if he had just left her.

WHAT A COWARD! She thought to herself, then immediately retracted the thought.

No, Malcolm loved her, she knew that. She wondered if he was dead, but felt that he was still alive. She believed this, and held on to the belief.

She was full of sadness as she climbed into the passenger seat of Pamela's 4-runner. She realized the search could not go on forever, but she felt that her husband was still out there – struggling to stay alive.

Chapter 75

Blythe meant to catch up on her reports, but at some point had fallen asleep at her desk. She awakened to the voice of a man speaking loudly in the hall outside her office. She sat up, pulled her desk mirror out of the drawer, and performed a quick self-assessment. Then she popped a mint into her mouth as she headed out into the hallway.

Don was talking on his mobile, "11 bodies and the 6 cadavers that you had sent over."

Don acknowledged Dr. Aspen's presence with a nod and raised eyebrows.

He continued, "We were able to get 33 clear prints that depicted at least 14 different people. I just sent the photos over to you. None of the bite marks on each of the bodies match. From what we have been able to discern, it looks like each killing was performed by a different person."

Blythe sat there as the horror of what Don had just said sinked in. She wondered what the Sheriff must be saying to him. She watched Don's facial expression for an indication.

"Yes sir, it very well could be a gang, maybe initiation, or we could still be looking at a new cult's ritual."

Don paused again. Blythe realized that her face was showing shock and fear. She quickly composed herself and waited for Don to finish his conversation.

"Very well, Sir. We'll be wrapping things up here and will return to HQ, ETA about 1 hour."

Don slid his finger across the screen of his smartphone, indicating the end of his conversation.

Blythe chimed in, "what do you think is going on, what'd the Sheriff say?"

"We do not know what is going on just yet. We are trying to put the pieces together. We still haven't heard from the FBI. Sheriff doesn't know what to think, except that he's worried that this just may be more widespread than any of us suspects right now. He's going to call other jurisdictions to find out if they are seeing anything similar. I think we were all hoping that it was one person doing all of this, the fact that we have more than a dozen killers with the same MO is extremely concerning."

"CONCERNING?! IT IS FREAKING SCARY!"

Blythe startled herself with her response. She had not meant to lose her composure. Don was staring at her and giving her a moment.

"Sorry, I am just stressed out, I am tired, and this whole nightmare is scaring the shit out of me."

"I understand, I have never seen or heard of something like this before. I am scared too," Don consoled.

Chapter 76

Sheriff Glasgow had just hung up the phone and instantly began barking orders.

He had 12 dead bodies with no identities that had apparently been eaten alive. He wondered how anybody could train for this scenario.

He called the department to order. Officers were going through a shift change, so there were plenty of cops in the house.

He announced, "Nobody is going home. At this time, overtime is approved and mandatory. We have an extremely serious situation going on here. I need everyone in the briefing room immediately and I need containment of the general public and press. MOVE!"

Instantly, the quiet room filled with action and noise. It sounded like an Elementary Cafeteria at lunchtime. The air filled with shouts, yelling, and scurrying. The public and press were ushered back into the lobby and outside. People were shouting and demanding answers.

The Sheriff watched his men and women in action. He heard the demands from the people and thought, *"You want to know what is going on? So do I."*

He hated how the press and public treated law enforcement as the bad guys. Anytime information wasn't readily available upon demand, accusations of cover-ups, corruption, and conspiracies sprung up like resurrection lilies.

Within 5 minutes, the people and press were ushered out, doors secured, and the officers began filing into the briefing room. Because of the number of officers now on duty, the room had to be cleared of the table and chairs in order to accommodate them.

It took another 5 minutes before the room was situated and the Sheriff was able to bring the room in to order. Officers were shoulder to shoulder with pens and notepads at the ready. All eyes were on the Sheriff.

The Sheriff began, "We do not have much to go on at the moment. What we do know is that we have 12 corpses without identities. Eleven of them appear to have been eaten, or at least bitten, to death."

The room seemed to gasp in unison.

The Sheriff continued with his briefing, "We have photos of their faces and the bite marks. It looks like we are dealing with 14 different assailants."

The room was no longer quiet. As the realization of the crimes being committed, the officers began discussing theories among themselves.

The Sheriff grew impatient and yelled, "SHUT-UP. THE MORE TIME WE SPEND IN HERE CHIT-CHATTING, THE MORE TIME WE ARE GIVING TO THESE GUYS TO CONTINUE CHOMPING

AND KILLING, NOW SETTLEDOWN AND LISTEN UP!"

The room instantly regained composure. The amount of respect the force had for the Sheriff was evident from the energy that existed in the room.

He continued, "It is looking like we are dealing with a group of assailants. This could be a gang or a cult. There is too much unknown. We are putting together packets of information as we speak. The packets include pictures, any details we have, and the locations of where the bodies were recovered. This is sensitive material and I do not want anybody who is not in this room to see any of it. Does everyone understand?"

Together the room shouted a resounding, "YES, SIR!"

"Some of the pictures are extremely graphic, so please brace yourselves. Simon, Baker, Phils, and Wilson: you will be notifying next of kin as soon as we find out who they are. We will need you to go to their home and transport them to and from the morgue for identification of the victims."

All four of them nodded their heads that they understood and accepted their assignments.

"Remain in contact with Missing Persons to see if any descriptions match our victims."

The nodding heads continued.

"Jameson, run over to dispatch and tell Deputy Maxton that we are going to need extra dispatchers. Have him call in the reserves and then set up a 'Call Out' for all Reserves, Volunteers, and Search and Rescue. Have them prepare for deployment. I am pulling out all the stops, I want this thing nipped in the butt before it gets any worse.

"We do not know what we are looking for, as of yet. I have a request for an FBI profiler, we'll update as information becomes available. For now, I want everyone to partner up, no one goes alone. We are going to canvass the county throughout the night. I want a heavy presence out there. I want the people to feel safe and secure. Look for anything suspicious and follow up on everything. At the moment, everything and anything is a lead.

"Jacob is passing around T-Cards. Fill them out and turn them in for your assignment. We are operating under the ICS model for now, follow your chain of command. Make sure you list on your T-Cards what your specialties are."

The T-Cards were appropriately named for their "T" shape. They were essentially name cards that organizers used to know who was available, to track, and to organize the troops. They are widely used by Search and Rescue Teams and FEMA during catastrophes or massive operations.

"Specifically we are looking for anyone chasing, chewing, biting, or fighting with an animal or a person. We have seen proof that pets are targets as well, but we fear that this has escalated to people. So continue to look for any of this.

"I want you to stop anyone who is roaming on the street and question them. If there is anything strange about the person, bring them in for questioning. Only arrest if there is cause. If you witness a group or a gang, call in for backup before approaching them. I want to corral the group. Make sure you get all of them. I do not want a chase, I would like for an organized surrounding and ambush.

"Because we are dealing with biters, protect yourselves. Practice BSI principles."

BSI, or Body Substance Isolation, referred to protecting oneself from the fluids of another. This involves the use of gloves, goggles, facemask, etc.

The Sheriff continued, "This is the point of the briefing where I would normally open this up to questions, but I have shared with you all that I know at this point. Plus, with this many people, we could easily be stuck here all night discussing this to death. I need you all on the streets to do any good. Keep your radios, computers, and phones on and charged. I want to avoid a panic but I also want to protect our own. So call your loved ones, tell them to stay indoors, with the doors and windows locked. This includes your pets. Do not give any details whatsoever. Do not talk to the press! Follow protocol, send the press here to speak to our Press Coordinator.

"Alright people, let's move."

Chapter 77

The President began banging on the table, but nobody seemed to respond. He got up from his seat, walked over to the door, and flicked the light switch on and off several times. The room instantly returned to silence. There were eyes of shame as the room regained composure and everyone returned to their seats.

The President addressed, "This is scary stuff. We are all worried and understandably upset. We fear for our safety, our family, and loved ones. Now is not the time to point fingers. Now is not the time to lose tempers. Now is not the time to abandon ship. Now is the time to rise to the occasion. Now is the time to fulfill our duties to the American People and the World. We are the leaders. We are the ones responsible and capable of addressing this problem. "We will follow protocol and do what it takes to retain order. The last thing we need is mass hysteria exacerbating the situation.

"Now, as I understand it, we have enough vaccine ready to administer to the top levels of government, next in line will be healthcare providers and military personnel. This will exhaust our current supplies. We are currently working on producing more vaccine, but this will take time. What I am proposing and asking for feedback on, is should we share this information with our allies? If we share this information, we can have labs around the world creating the vaccine and producing it for distribution around the world. This is typically how we have addressed shortages in the past. Before we open this to discussion, please realize the potential for this turning into a biological weapon. If this is released, it will more than likely become available to our enemies. I can foresee this potentially being used against us."

The room fell completely silent as the occupants contemplated the ramifications of a biological weapon where citizens were eating each other.

The President continued, "there is still the probability that the influenza and demand for meat are unrelated. This could just be paranoia. We just do not know, yet. But I for one, do not want to wait for this to become a major pandemic problem. I say we mass produce the vaccines, push for everyone's vaccination, and hope for the best."

Many offered their agreements with grunts and head nods.

The Doctor interrupted, "Yes, that is good, but the problem is that the vaccine only addresses the influenza. It is not designed to address the Carnivorous Bacterialus."

"But by stopping the influenza, we address the mode of transport of this virus or bacteria, correct," Secretary of Defense William Docern questioned.

"Yes, in theory, that is correct," the Doctor replied.

"Well, Mr. President, I suggest that as a matter of human welfare we open the creation of the vaccines to the rest of the world. But, as a matter of National Security, we keep the facts and theories of this Carnivorous Bacterialus under wraps," Mr. Docern offered.

Chapter 78

James moved his family down to Southern Arizona shortly after buying a large ranch in preparation for Y2K. At the time, he did not believe that Y2K was real or that it would amount to the predicted chaos. What James feared most was the reaction of the masses to the fear of Y2K. The scariest aspect of any major catastrophe was how the people reacted. James believed that these major events brought out the best in some, but the worst of most.

Anticipating the worst, James purchased the ranch south of Tucson, near the Mexican Border. Originally, he stocked the ranch with enough supplies to support his family for a few months. He believed that the government would regain control of society within a month, since he was removed from a major city, he allowed the buffer of an extra two months.

After 9-11, James became obsessive with protecting his family and his land. He began acquiring various armaments. He dug a bunker that was accessible through a hidden door from inside the house. The bunker was constructed out of two shipping containers that he had buried side by side.

From the bunker he had dug a long tunnel that exited behind a mound of boulders and a small hill. The tunnel was where he stored most of his provisions. On either side of the tunnel were shelves from floor to ceiling, stocked with cans and bottles of food, medical supplies, extra ammo, barrels of water, and fuel.

As James could afford to do so, he fortified his location. When he purchased his property, barbed-wire fencing already surrounded it. He added two more fences between the border and his house. The inner circle encompassed 5 acres, where his house, bunker, barn, water-tank, and garden existed.

The middle ring was where he raised livestock: cows, goats, and llamas. The outer-ring he allowed to go wild, acting as a buffer to the outside world. He hoped that the empty land would convince others that nothing valuable existed beyond the fence.

Chapter 79

Malcolm was starving and constantly cold. He had lost track of time, but he figured that it must be late October or early November. He based this on the snow that had began falling a couple weeks prior. He was able to sustain himself by hunting animals and occasionally stealing from other hunters, but he had not seen another human being in quite sometime.

Once the rain and snow began to fall, the Forest Service closed off the dirt roads leading to the trailheads. Nobody visited the forest during the winter months.

Malcolm was growing weary and began doubting the intelligence of his decision to stay in the forest. He had consumed all the fuel in his lighter. His batteries had died in all of his electronics; flashlight, GPS, and Spot. Fortunately, he had his back up, a battery free flashlight, which gained power by shaking the light vigorously.

He hadn't been able to locate or kill an animal in about a week. It seemed that they had all migrated or gone into hibernation. Malcolm wandered the forest, searching for substance. He was tired, cold, hungry, miserable, and above all... he missed his wife.

Every night he would gaze at the middle star of Orion's belt. Every night he would wonder how Brenda was doing, wondering if she still looked at the same star. Depression would set in each night that clouds prevented him from seeing the star.

He thought about going back, trying to explain things to her. But how do you explain putting your wife through so much stress, anxiety, and depression? How could she possibly ever understand, let alone forgive him? No matter how much his heart ached for her, he knew that he could never go back.

As his hunger increased, Malcolm's cravings became more intense. He had begun having nightmares of eating humans. On occasion he would awake in night terror drenched sweat, after dreaming of seeing Brenda's face on the body that he had been feasting on.

No, for her sake – and everyone else – he could not go back. It would be best if he just stayed out in the forest until he met his Maker.

Chapter 80

Officers and detectives began to scurry out of the room. They filed into the hallway where a "Sign-In" table had been erected. Here they turned in their T-Cards. Next they made their way to the cafeteria/break room that was transformed into a staging area to await assignments.

They did not have to wait too long; assignments were given as quickly as people entered the room. Two by two, the teams and assignments were yelled out. As soon as the names were uttered, the officers responded and took their assignment package and then they were off.

Sheriff Glasgow was extremely please to see the trainings payoff. The machine moved smoothly. Within 30 minutes, all of the assignments were given and the forces were departing. Since the 9-11 terrorist attacks, the department had regular trainings. Not only did they train for a massive terrorist attack, but also for a major natural disaster. The trainings covered every imaginable scenario. The theory was to prepare for the worst scenario and thus be ready for anything. So far, it worked seamlessly.

Sheriff called out for Miller as he made his way for his office. Miller immediately stopped his conversation and quickly fell in step behind his superior. While Glasgow was usually easy going, he also ran a tight ship. He was extremely fair, demanded respect, and equally deposited respect and praise on his subordinates. The entire force respected and supported him. The tight knit camaraderie of the force provided Glasgow the confidence in knowing that he could count on anyone of them for anything that he needed.

Miller closed the door behind him as he followed Glasgow into his office. Glasgow sat behind his desk and Miller stood at attention with his hands clasped behind his back and waited for the Sheriff to speak.

"I need you to contact all of the Chaplains that we have available and have them report to the Morgue. Tell them that we will be sending next of kin down there to identify their loved ones. I want them down there to offer whatever services and support they may need. Make sure you brief them on the situation and do not sugar coat it one bit. I want them fully aware and prepared. Make sure that they protect their loved ones, but express the importance of keeping this under wrap. Got it?"

"Yes, Sir. I'm on it. Anything else?" Miller asked.

"Yes, send in Carquinez."

The Sheriff could hear Miller shout for Carquinez louder than needed. He had lungs, but always over used them. The rookie was too anxious to please, but Glasgow could not fault him too much for that.

Carquinez wrapped his bony knuckle on the open door. Glasgow said come in without looking up.

"Sam, I need to prepare a public announcement without giving away too much detail. I do not want public chaos. Put together a statement that urges people to secure themselves and their pets indoors at night until this thing blows over. Tell them that the police have things under control and that patrols have been doubled. Invite the public to promptly report any suspicious activities. Write this up right away and bring it to me before talking to the press. Send Jacob out to inform the press that a statement is in the process of being prepared and will be delivered shortly. He is not to divulge any information or take any questions. There is to be no Q&A at this time. Alright, get on it."

Carquinez performed a perfect about face and quickly left the office.

Next thing on his agenda was to contact Blythe.

Chapter 81

"Dr. Aspen," Blythe stated as she answered the phone. She did not even look at the caller ID, just pushed the button on her earpiece.

"Blythe, it's Glasgow. How you holding out there?"

"Oh, the usual, tired and grumpy with a load of dead bodies. What can I do for you?"

"Well, as soon as we can identify the bodies, I'll be bringing over the next of kin to confirm identities. Are you good, or would you like me to send someone to relieve you?"

"I'm ok, I planned on staying through the night anyway. I prefer spending the night with the dead to my rowdy neighbors," Blythe replied.

Blythe lived alone in a condo. She loved the place, until the girls moved in downstairs. They were young. Two sisters; one 23 and the other 21. They had friends in and out of their place at all hours of the day and night. The partying never seemed to end.

Not having air conditioning, Blythe liked to leave her windows open. Their endless smoking prevented her from any fresh air.

She suspected drug use, being that they never seemed to sleep. She had called the cops on numerous occasions. Over the course of 4 months, the girls had quite a rap sheet of complaints to the police and the HOA. Unfortunately, all they got were letters and warnings to keep it down. Blythe was forced to suffer.

"Alright. Heads up, I am sending the cavalry. I have ordered that Chaplains report to your location to be there for the families. Also, I suspect that we will have more bodies on their way before the night ends," Glasgow informed.

"Yeah, I was thinking the same thing, but somehow hearing you say it sends a chill down my spine. I am running out of room down here, can you come get these animal carcasses out of here?" Blythe requested with a demanding tone.

"You bet, I'll send Deputy Stevens with the wagon right away. We've got Togo's sandwiches here, you hungry?" the Sheriff offered.

"Yes, I am starving. I will take whatever you have to offer."

"Sure, anything else?"

"Yeah, I was wondering if you were able to ID any of the perps by their dental records?"

"No. Unfortunately, there is no dental database available. They are not like fingerprints. Bite-marks and dental records are not usually used to find people, but sometimes they are used to convict criminals. It would take a court order to obtain dental records, and that is only useful if we already have an idea of the perp and which dentist she or he frequents. We are inputting the victims fingerprints into the system to try and identify them, so far, no hits."

"Ok. Well keep up the good work. I will be here if you need me."

Chapter 82

Jonathan had spent countless days searching the Internet for clues to explain the President's behavior. He would stay up most nights chatting with co-conspirator theorist. At 2:30 am, he was about to retire to his bed. As he reached to turn off his monitor, his computer rang out with a ding that informed him of a new message.

He grabbed his mouse, located the cursor over the blinking bar, and clicked.

The chat instantly opened into a screen that engulfed one-fifth of his screen.

It was Sachi who had sent him a message:

"Have you seen the latest press release from WHO on the new virus?"

"No. Why? What's up? I was just about to go to bed."

"I think this will keep you up tonight."

Sachi included a link to the article after his last post.

Jonathan sighed and clicked on the link.

New virus identified in France, linked to coronavirus

The Health Protection Agency (HPA) has confirmed a fifth case in relation to this new strain of the menacing coronavirus. The coronavirus, which causes the common cold, is also the source of outbreaks such as SARS (Severe Acute Respiratory Syndrome).

The latest, of two cases to plague Europe, is a patient who traveled to Israel. The previous case was in UK, a patient who recently had traveled to Egypt. The other three cases are being reported in Tokyo, Delhi, and Sao Paulo.

A laboratory in the UK first discovered the strain. The laboratory performed routine blood work on a patient who complained of a change of appetite, eating behaviors, and sleep eating.

The findings of the new strain were confirmed in the reports from the four related cases.

It does not appear that this strain is cause for alarm, as no confirmed deaths have been associated with the strain. Still, the WHO is concerned that this strain is wide spread and has the probability of evolving.

The origins for this virus are, at the moment, unknown. It is believed to have begun in Delhi, where the first documented case resides.

What is most baffling to researchers is that the new strain does not appear to be killing victims, but appears to alter receptors in the brain that increases the appetite. More specifically, the appetite increases cravings for meat.

World Health officials are concerned that the findings suggest that the Coronavirus is taking on new forms that could be cause for alarm. Traditionally, Coronavirus attacks the respiratory system and is transferred through direct contact, sneezing, coughing, etc.

There is no cure, just treatments for the coronavirus. Nor is there a vaccine for this strain. Health officials are encouraging individuals and health providers to take normal precautions. Wash hands frequently, cover coughs and sneezes, and stay home if you are sick.

WHO is encouraging all health providers to report findings of this new strand to aid in the tracking and research of this evolving virus.

The World Health Organization and the European Centre for Disease Control report that there is no immediate cause for alarm.

As there are only five known cases, none of which have died, there is no specific evidence of an ongoing threat. The public should continue going about their lives. There is no specific advice to travellers. Simply, continue to take recommended precautions to avoid infections. Further advice to the public and health officials will be given as soon as information becomes available.

Jonathan leaned back in his office chair. He interlaced his fingers behind his head.

He wondered, *"Could this be connected to the President pushing for the Flu Vaccinations? It seems like a stretch, but maybe he knows something that he isn't sharing with the world."*

Chapter 83

Malcolm determined, by way of his worn map, that he was between 6 and 8 thousand feet in elevation. He decided that he would need to descend below the snow line if he hoped to have any chance of surviving.

He had with him a warm coat and a descent bag and tent, but he was not outfitted for winter conditions. His tent was not a rated 4-season, the last high wind had snapped both of the main poles. He continued to use the tent for makeshift shelters.

Malcolm began heading southwest toward Yosemite National Park. He considered heading back the way he had come, but figured that the many passes would be difficult to cross. Besides, surely his truck had been towed away. Even if it was still there, it would likely be snowed in. Besides, the gates to the highway would be closed for winter. He would perish long before he could find any kind of support.

A mixture of snow and rain continued to fall. The sleet came sideways at his face as he hiked. The wind made every attempt of pushing him off the side of the trail. He struggled to maintain his course.

The heavy downfall and cloud cover made it impossible to obtain any sort of bearing. It was impossible to see the mountain ranges that surrounded him.

There was little point in referencing the map without a point of reference. Instead, Malcolm marched on with his body hunched over, head close to the ground, and his hands shielding his eyes from the sleet.

Malcolm concentrated his focus on the trail. He continued bearing into the oncoming wind. Each step was a concerted effort of will, determination, and brut strength.

Because of the dark overcast, it was difficult to determine the time of day. He could not estimate the time of day based on hunger, because he was constantly hungry.

Thankfully, he wore Gore Tex boots, which had kept his feet dry during creek crossings. But now, his feet were constantly wet with sweat, as the material refused to let the moisture out. He constantly worried about his feet. If he failed to properly care for his feet, he would perish quickly.

His mind thought of the history special he watched about World War I. Many soldiers lost their feet and lives to Trench foot; a condition that occurs when feet are constantly wet. Trapped inside moist boots, fungus thrives and literally eats the skin of the foot. The foot becomes infected with gangrene and requires amputation. If the soldier did not die from the gangrene, he had a good possibility of dying from infection from the amputation.

After hiking for several hours, Malcolm located a tree well beneath a large pine tree. He used what little energy he had left, to hollow out the hole. He built a roof shelter over head with fresh pine limbs. He dug into the frozen ground and broke off roots from the tree. He stuck these in his mouth and chewed on them as he continued to build his shelter.

After lining the ground with several inches of pine needles, Malcolm set off to find firewood. He trampled through 6 inches of newly fallen snow. He thanked the heavens for the calm break in the storm. Everything was peaceful and quiet.

He gathered up armfuls of dead wood and returned to his location. He dug a second hole for his fire, just outside his shelter. With snow and branches, he built up a windscreen that protected his fire from the wind and also acted as a reflector to direct the heat inward.

Exposing the filaments, Malcolm carefully removed the glass of the light bulb from his flashlight. He shook the flashlight for several seconds. Then he carefully lowered this down to his kindling. He had made a pile of shredded material - mostly pine fur. He touched the filaments to the pile and flipped on the switch. A spark was instantly created between the filaments, but failed to take off.

Malcolm continued trying to get the fire started - his life literally depended on this. The skies were darkening, indicating that either it was the end of the day or that a serious storm was brewing. On the 13th attempt, the spark took.

"Lucky number 13", he said aloud to himself.

He carefully put his face down near the premature flame. He shielded the pile with his hands and gingerly blew. The flame took to life and grew slowly. The flame struggled against the moist surroundings, producing mostly white smoke.

Fueling the fire, he began adding pieces of timber; each addition, slowly progressing in size. Finally, he was able to place a full log into the fire. With constant nursing, the log began to burn and produce a modest flame.

Malcolm relished in the minute amount of warmth produced from his meager fire.

He continued to nurse the fire. Eventually, he was able to advance the fire to a three-log furnace. He carefully removed his shoes and socks, placing them over a branch near the fire. He stretched out his legs, hovering his feet as near to the flame as he could stand.

He alternated rubbing each foot as the heat became unbearable. His hands spread the heat around on the soles of his abused feet. He found amusement in the thought of walking into a salon and requesting a pedicure for his dirty and mangled feet.

Once he had his feet under control, he turned his mind back to food and water that his body desperately needed. He sipped from the cup of melting snow that he placed near the fire.

He reached up into the tree branches above and pulled off a couple of pinecones. He broke open the cones and consumed the nuts. He threw the rest of the cones into the fire. He enjoyed the sound of the crackling as the cones burst and burned.

Malcolm squirmed into his sleeping bag. He was hungry and thirsty, but at least he was warm. He drifted off as he gazed into the roaring flames of the fire he had built.

Chapter 84

Stevenson and Millard were assigned the Parks neighborhood, a subdivision that was built in the late 1960's. The track homes stretched four miles along a major freeway and covered 10 square miles of winding roads, parks, and two schools. The subdivision was named the Parks because each of the streets was named after a national park.

The neighborhood went through various stages over the years. In the beginning, it was typical suburbia. In the late 70's and early 80's, hippies and drug use overran the parks. Stevenson grew up in the Parks and remembers playing on the playground while older kids were smoking pot and lying under the nearby trees.

By the late 80's the hippies were replaced by Latino gangs. The gangs terrorized the neighborhood, leaving their mark via graffiti on anything stationary. Parents no longer allowed their kids to play in the parks and the values deteriorated.

At the turn of the century, the police force obtained additional funding. The Parks benefitted by the influx of funds. Increased and dedicated patrols played apart in reducing the crime.

Neighborhood watch programs were implemented. The city replaced old playgrounds with updated equipment. Children returned to the parks and the neighborhood entered into a new phase.

Stevens and Millard made their rounds, taking time to carefully examine the schoolyards and parks.

Stevenson was driving, while Millard was occasionally operating the spotlight. As they passed by Rix Park, Millard spotted movement.

"Hold it," Millard ordered.

Stevenson braked the car to a stop and he scanned their surroundings.

Millard saw the dark shapes of a group of guys walking through the park, making their way away from their position. As far as Millard could tell, the group had not scene the squad car.

"Do you see that group moving away from us," Millard inquired?

"Yeah, I see them. Call it in; we'll pull around to the other end of the park. How many did you make out?"

"I counted four, maybe more."

"Call for backup, just encase any of them decide to make a run for it."

"Right. Dispatch – R368."

"Go for R368"

"We are at the Southern end of Rix Park in the Parks Subdivision. We made a visual on a group heading North on foot through the park. We are currently in route to the Northern end of the park to intercept and make contact. Requesting assistance. Over."

"10-4, R368. Available units near the Parks Subdivision, please respond to assist unit at the Northern end of Rix Park. Hawk Team 3, provide aerial support."

"Dispatch, R814 in route, responding to Rix Park, over."

"10-4, R814, proceed with caution, no lights or sirens."

"Hawk Team 3 responding. ETA 2 minutes."

"10-4, Hawk Team 3."

"R368, maintain visual of suspect group and wait for assistance before proceeding."

"10-4."

Chapter 85

Stevenson and Millard's heartbeats sped up as the adrenalin increased in their bodies anticipating the possible encounter. Stevenson quickly drove to the other end of the park and slowed the vehicle to a stop in the shadows of a large Maple tree. From where they had stopped they no longer had a visual, they sat and waited for the group to appear.

They did not see the helicopter approach overhead, but they jumped to attention as soon as the floodlight turned night into day.

"Shit!" Millard yelled.

Within seconds a group of guys came running toward the edge of the park. The radio sprang to life as Hawk Team 3 gave a play-by-play from their vantage point in the sky.

"Hawk Team 3 has visual on group of suspects. Suspects are on the move, heading north. Stay awake fellows, group is aware of our presence and beginning to spread out. We count 5 suspects. Over."

Millard yelled, "Go! Go! Go!"

Stevenson reacted by pulling his vehicle into the residential street and flipping the switches on for the vehicles' light bar. The line of houses on either side of the street came alive with alternating red and blue hues. Millard fired up the spot light and flooded the street.

Three guys instantly shielded their eyes with raised arms. They were dressed in dark clothes and carrying various weapons: a bat, a rifle, and a golf club.

Millard barked into the PA system, "Freeze! Sheriff's Department! Put down your weapons!"

One of the guys immediately dropped the golf club that he was carrying, while the other two spun around and began running in the opposite direction. R814 unfortunately drove up to the scene from the same direction and failed to close off the exit points.

"Damn it," Millard managed to get out as he leapt from the vehicle.

He gave chase after the group, shoving the remaining guy to the ground as he ran passed him. Stevenson followed and slapped cuffs on the downfallen suspect.

R814 threw their vehicle in reverse and backed away from the scene. They flipped the vehicle around and sped through the neighborhood in Code 3.
The radio awakened. Hawk Team 3 gave the play by play.

"Group has split up! Officers are giving chase. Suspects are armed, I repeat, suspects are armed! Two guys are now running up Yellowstone, one guy backtracking South through Rix Park, and fourth guy hopped a fence on Everglades and is now running Southwest down the flood canal. We need reinforcements now!"

"10-4," The dispatcher chimed in. "All available units please respond to the Parks Subdivision. Be on the lookout for armed suspects."

Chapter 86

Waking up to a brisk breeze slapping his face, Malcolm laid shivering. He wondered how long he had been asleep. He stared at what had been his roaring fire. Unburned timber sat inches from the fire pit. If only he had woken in time to add more logs.

Why couldn't the logs just magically place themselves into the flames?

He lifted his head, stretched his sore aching back and examined his fortress. A snowdrift had built up against one side, further protecting him from the harsh elements.

He could hear the occasional howling of wind rush through the tree branches above.

Breaking open another pinecone, he consumed the nuts. Then he went about rebuilding his fire. It was vital that he regain hydration, for this he needed the heat to melt the snow.

He had filled the Jet Boil pot with snow. It was obvious that it had turned to water and then frozen.

Once he got the fire going and water in his system, he moved out to seek food.

Noticing chipmunk tracks around his shelter, he realized that he was not the only one living off the nuts. He took his shoelaces and parachute cord to fashion snare traps. He placed them along the tracks. He also fashioned a few large rocks to fall on the critters. He enticed the rodents with piles of pine nuts.

After setting a good dozen traps, Malcolm felt satisfied with his odds.

He then decided to follow the tracks of a rabbit. He crossed the snow, careful to periodically look up to obtain bearings. He had heard of countless mushroom hunters in Mendocino county who became lost after walking for miles with their noses to the ground.

He followed the tracks up and over boulders, through brush, and across a frozen stream. Several times the tracks disappeared, a result of the wind blowing across the snow. This made Malcolm wonder how fresh the tracks were.

He continued to follow the tracks until - once again - they disappeared. He stood looking around for the continuation, but could not find them anywhere. Just as he was about to turn around, he noticed that the tracks ended near a pile of rocks. Upon closer examinations, he noticed a small hole that was burrowed underneath Manzanita brush.

Malcolm set up a blind next to the Manzanita. He used 10 feet of parachute cord to fashion a lasso that he positioned around the hole. Then he sat behind his blind and patiently waited.

Chapter 87

Millard loved a good chase. Most cops complained when a perp took off, making them run. He loved it. He had always loved running and racing. Through high school and college, he ran track and cross-country. Even with all his gear, he never had a problem catching a perp who was running away from him.

After slamming the one guy to the ground, as he passed, he selected the next closest guy and honed in. The guy had a good 35-yard head start on him. The challenge brought Millard to life. He chased the guy down Everglades and never paused for a second when he saw the guy scale the 7-foot chain-link fence into the flood canal.

Millard used his moment, leaping toward the top of the fence. His abdomen and feet hit at the same time. His stomach connected with the top of the fence, he buckled over the fence, grabbed the chain-link on the opposing side, and simultaneously pulled with his arms while donkey kicking his legs. The result was a seamless somersault over the fence with a mid-stride landing. He continued to run with his focus trained on the guy in front of him.

The perfect fence crossing had help shorten the gap. The suspect was now a mere 15 yards in front of him. He remained focus, making sure he was breathing properly, his arms moving in perfect rhythm and alignment.

At 10 yards away from his target, Millard fired what his coaches had referred to as his afterburners. This was a release of all he had left in his tanks. When the finish line was within reach, he opened it all up.

Instantly Millard was 5 yards away. This was coming within the danger zone; an area where the perp could easily spin around and deliver a sucker-punch or fire a deadly shot on his pursuer.

Each time Millard entered the danger zone his mind flashed back to the day when he learned the tough lesson of the danger zone. He was 6 years old. He was chasing a bully who had pushed his friend down and then taken off. Millard quickly caught up to him, but just as he was about to tackle the guy, the bully spun around and gave Millard his first broken nose.

Millard closed in on the perp and watched for any sudden movement indicating a defensive strike. Two yards from the guy, Millard prepared to reach out and grab the guy. Just as he was lifting his arms, he saw the guy's body shift. Millard crouched as he leapt forward. The perp's bat swished over Millard's head.

Millard launched all 190 pounds of his body into the mid-section of the assailant. They both crumpled to the ground. Millard grunted as they went down and he heard all of the air rush out of the assailant.

As they hit the ground, their bodies rolled down the dirt embankment and into the slosh of mud and cattails. The assailant struggled to his feet, back kicked Millard catching him on the right shoulder, and made another attempt to escape. As the assailant began to run, Millard dove for his back foot and managed to trip the guy. He went face first into the mud. Before he could recover, Millard was on his back, making sure every orifice was filled with the stench of the creek.

Millard cuffed and dragged the guy up the side of the creek and marched him back to the Everglades crossing.

Chapter 88

"Suspects on Everglades and flood canal have been apprehended," the guys in Hawk 3 announced. "We have as much of the area lit up as possible. We have one guy making his way through the shadows of Rix Park, heading South. The two guys heading up Yellowstone have split up. One took a left on Yosemite and the other continued straight on Yellowstone."

The two officers in the helicopter could see the other squad cars entering the subdivision, but the guys were spreading out and they couldn't keep an eye on all of them. They had to make a decision. Pilot Jacobsen went with the guy in the park, hoping that Squad Car R814 could cut off the guy on Yellowstone.

The Pilot lit up the area where he last saw the guy duck into the shadows of a tree. He could not make out any movement or body. They hovered overhead, then he tried small circles to get different angles. Jacobsen became frustrated when he could not see the guy and realized that the others were out of his sight now as well.

He saw a squad car pull up into the park and begin sweeping with a floodlight. Jacobsen ascended higher into the sky and illuminated half the park. The guy must be hiding or somehow got through the park. Jacobsen flew around the adjacent streets and lit up the backyards of homes. Nothing was moving.

"Dispatch, this is Hawk Team 3."

"Go for Hawk Team 3."

"We no longer have a visual on the remaining perps, over."

"10-4. What do you advise, over."

"We are going to continue surveillance from up here, but we need to contain the situation. We need squad cars to head off the main exits from the area."

"Roger that. Responding units, cordon and set up check points at Hilo, Seneca, Kings, and Regents."

Over the next several hours, the Subdivision of the Parks neighborhood looked like a war zone. The neighborhood was swarming with patrol cars, K9 units, and foot patrols. Hawk Team 3 had to leave for refueling and was replaced with Hawk Team 1.

The Sheriff decided that their resources were all tied up in the neighborhood and nothing was happening. So he called off the dogs and focused his attention on the two men that they had in custody.

Chapter 89

Hours went by as Malcolm watched the clouds build up and then disperse. Fortunately, the weather was cooperating, for now. He tried to remain as quiet as possible. He sat cross-legged until his legs began to fall asleep.

Refusing to move, he allowed the cut-off circulation to turn to pins and needles in his legs. He was then forced to reposition. He found it painful and difficult to stretch out his legs. He pulled at them with his arms, as if he were moving somebody else's legs. Finally stretched out, he sighed a quiet sigh of relief.

The blood returning to his legs was as –or more- painful as the pins and needles. Malcolm stuck a twig in his mouth and clamped down. He looked at the Manzanita, willing it to produce berries. In the dead of winter, the scrub did not even have leaves that he could make tea with.

Malcolm held his breath as he caught movement out of the corner of his eye. He tried desperately to stay still. A rabbit's head peered out of the hole. The little nose was twitching, as he examined the air for the scent of any threats.

Malcolm continued to hold his breath, hoping that the rabbit would not smell or hear him. The rabbit suddenly darted back into the hole.

Malcolm felt deflated and he let the air escape his lungs. He was about to throw in the towel when the rabbit's head reappeared. The rabbit investigated the air again, but this time he sniffed around the perimeter of his entry.

With his heart beating harder and harder, Malcolm prayed that the parachute cord would not bother the rabbit. The rabbit's head darted back into the hole, then just as quickly reappeared.

His nose was twitching, his whiskers struggling to keep up. The animal looked up, side to side, and up again.

Malcolm readjusted his fingers on the cord. He was poised to act on a moments notice. The rabbit pulled back slightly into the hole, and then without warning sprung forward.

Malcolm yanked on the cord as hard and fast as his fatigued body could muster. Everything happened so fast, he was not able to watch it all unfold. He turned his head back to the hole to find the rabbit struggling to free itself.

The rabbit almost had made it; the cord barely caught one of his hind legs. The rabbit rolled, kicked, and tried chewing through the cord.

Malcolm yanked on the cord again causing the rabbit to sprawl out. Then he lifted the rabbit into the air, the creature struggled to find freedom from his capture.

With a pine branch that he had been using as a walking stick, Malcolm swung at the rabbit's head. He connected, but merely grazed the animal.

The rabbit let loose a terrible screech. It sounded to Malcolm like a child that was in serious pain. The sound was so terrible that it motivated Malcolm to swing repeatedly just to get it to stop.

Finally, the noise stopped and Malcolm lashed the rabbit to his club and followed his tracks back.

Chapter 90

Though he was on the brink of starving to death, Malcolm immediately tended to his dying fire. He dropped the load of wood he had gathered on his way back and propped the rabbit up by plunging his stick into the snow.

Once the fire was roaring again, Malcolm gutted and skinned the rabbit. He threw all of the innards into his Jet Boil mug and set it near the fire. The meat, he ate raw after drinking the blood he had gathered into his squishy cup.

He added snow, bones, and pine needles to his innards-soup. He let it boil, continually adding snow as it melted. Though he had to fight every urge within him, he saved half of the rabbit and had it cut into strips. These, he placed over the fire for drying. He planned on rationing and making this meat last as long as possible.

After eating and resting, Malcolm was feeling much better. He pulled out his map and made an attempt at discovering where he was. There was nothing substantial that he could pinpoint that he could confer with on the map.

Malcolm crawled out of his shelter and walked around to gather more wood and check his snares.

He was frustrated to find the nuts missing from three of his snares. Then he saw the large boulder had fallen. He rushed over - crossing his fingers - he lifted the rock.

Beneath the rock was a smashed chipmunk, chewed pine nuts spewed from his tiny snout. Feeling bad and at the same time grateful, Malcolm scooped up the little guy and carried him back to his fire.

As he returned to his shelter, he saw a coyote darting between trees.

"Great, just what I need. Don't you go thinking that you are going to steal my food without a fight," Malcolm shouted.

He wondered how he could kill the coyote, knowing that without a gun it would be nearly impossible. Snares were useless, the cousins to the canine were known for chewing their own legs off. They were too quick to catch or club. Malcolm envisioned himself spearing the dog, as if he had any of the necessary skill.

Out of ideas, Malcolm used his knife to sharpen the ends of four straight branches. He placed the shavings near the fire, so he could use them should the fire die down again.

Malcolm made the most of the little rodent, he added his tiny organs to his boiling stew. Then he placed the little guy on a stick and slowly roasted him over the fire.

With the daylight quickly fading, Malcolm prepared for the night. He figured that he would not be obtaining much shuteye with the coyote out there, so he made provisions for getting the dog.

He dangled the meat from the chipmunk on a shoelace held six feet off the ground. Then he secured one of his spears to a branch of the pine tree. He pulled the branch back and tied it off with a cord that led back to his shelter. The branch was poised to swing the spear directly under the dangling meat.

As a back up plan, he buried a snare trap beneath the snow that was attached to the meat. If the coyote managed to get the meat, he would set off the snare. Then Malcolm would have to run out and club the animal.

That night, each time Malcolm dozed off, he would hear footsteps. He could hear the dog pacing outside the light of his fire. He kept the fire going, keeping warm inside his shelter.

Occasionally, he caught a glimpse of the coyote as he danced in the shadows. He tried desperately to track the movements, to keep a tab on the animal's whereabouts, but it moved too fast and stealthy.

Hours went by, as the coyote waited for Malcolm to fall asleep. Malcolm kept his peripheral on the hanging remains of the chipmunk. Each time he would wake, he would check the rodent, and then add another log to the fire.

Malcolm decided that he had overstayed his welcome in this location. If he didn't catch the coyote, he would have to move on in the morning. He couldn't go another sleepless night out here. He needed his rest.

Chapter 91

Sheriff Glasgow watched the interrogation from behind the one-way mirror. Deputy Millard sat calmly across the metal table from Paul. Stevenson entered the room and presented the Dixie cup of water that Paul had requested.

It was obvious that Paul was nervous, though he tried his best to maintain his tough guy exterior façade.

Stevenson leaned up against the wall behind Paul, a tactic that he used to keep a suspect uneasy and guessing.

Millard spoke first, "What were you guys doing out there, roaming around in the middle of the night?"

"Nothing, just hangin," Paul responded.

Paul was surprisingly clean cut. He was a tall blond, good-looking kid. His driver's license revealed that he was 24 years old.

"If you weren't doing anything, what was with the weapons?"

Paul shrugged, "Rough neighborhood."

"Ok, if you are innocent, then you have nothing to hide. So who were you with?"

Millard knew that he was revealing that they hadn't apprehended everyone, but he had to try and get the names of those that had gotten away. Paul had a mixture of elation and regret upon hearing that some of the guys got away. He analyzed in his mind what went wrong. He couldn't figure out how the cop had caught up to him so quickly.

Paul refused to respond. He wondered who had gotten away. All he saw was Kyle sitting in the back of a patrol car as Officer 'Speedy Gonzalez' escorted him back up Everglades.

Millard continued, "Look, we got you some water. We are being nice here, and believe me we don't have to be. So why don't you keep the peace and start answering some questions? How many of you were there?"

Paul remained silent with a stone cold look on his face. He wondered how Kyle was holding up and hoped that he wasn't spilling his guts, but suspected that he would.

"Listen Paul, we got you roaming streets at night in a gang with weapons. This is an intent to cause harm to others or destruction to property. We can charge you with evading officers of the law, resisting arrest, and assault on an officer. Officer Stevenson is a real creative guy, I'm sure he can double the charges, couldn't you?"

Stevenson chimed in, "Oh, easily. How about interfering with an official investigation, crime against animals, theft, and several counts of murder."

Millard thought Stevenson was revealing too much and going overboard, but Paul shifted in his seat revealing his discomfort.

"So, what are you going to tell us," Millard inquired.

Paul finally broke his silence, "I didn't kill nobody, I didn't commit any crime against no animals, and I didn't steal anything. You are fishing and trying to scare me. I have not done anything wrong. Can I get something to clean my face from when you shoved my face in the mud and nearly suffocated me?"

Millard went red and kicked his chair back against the wall behind him as he leaned his body across the table. His face was inches from Paul's.

Paul could feel the warm breath blowing from Millard's nostrils. He braced himself for a blow that would result in a case of police brutality.

Stevenson stood at attention and ready to react if Millard completely lost his temper.

Sheriff Glasgow's voice erupted from the speaker, "Gentlemen, can I speak with you for a moment?"

Stevenson walked around the table and pulled Millard away. Paul smiled and further aggravated Millard. Stevenson coaxed him to leave the room.

Chapter 92

Millard erupted into the side room where the Sheriff was waiting.

"What the hell? This dude is playing tough ball, why? He's got to be guilty, he's hiding everything," Millard argued.

"Guys," the Sheriff began. "This kid has no record. He has never so much as shoplifted. We have nothing and he is not giving us anything. Let him sweat it out for awhile and go question his buddy."

"Should we leave him in there alone? He might try and walk out, we haven't charged him with anything officially," Stevenson offered.

"No, go in and slap the cuffs back on him. Turn the recorder on and give him the Miranda jingle again. Charge him with evading police, resisting arrest, and assault of an officer. Do not respond to whatever he says, just escort him to a cell and then lets question the other guy. I am in the process of obtaining a court order to obtain both of their dental impressions."

"Sir, we could shock him with photos of the corpses, see how he reacts," Stevenson suggested.

"No, let's question the other guy and then we'll consider doing that. I do not want to show them all of our cards. Honestly, we do not even know if these are the guys we are looking for. The real problem could still be out there. These guys may just be delinquents wondering the streets at night," the Sheriff reasoned.

Chapter 93

The officers returned to the interrogation room and performed just as the Sheriff had instructed. Paul began shaking and yelling that he was ready to cooperate.

They escorted him to a cell and removed his handcuffs. He stood at the bars and wondered what would be next.

Then he saw the officers escorting Kyle by his cell. Kyle looked shaken and scared. He looked at Paul for a brief second before one of the cops forcibly turned his head and urged him forward with a shove to the back.

Paul took a seat on the stainless steel bench. The coldness of the steel immediately stole the warmth from his body through his jeans. He sat on top of his hands to shield the further loss of warmth. His body shivered to maintain warmth. He lowered his face into his shoulder and tried fruitlessly to remove the dried on mud from his face.

As he sat there he allowed himself to realize that he had never been in trouble with the law. This was the first time he had even personally seen a cell, minus his 6th grade field trip to Alcatraz. He had been in numerous fights, had stolen things occasionally, and there was that night when he and Dillon had taken care of the Afghan Gang Bangers, but he had never been caught. He actually never even had so much as a speeding ticket.

"Crap, there goes my reputation," he joked to himself. He could always count on his sense of humor!

His mind then went over the 'discussion' in the interrogation room. The cops had mentioned charging him with animal cruelty and murder!

Were they serious or merely fishing and trying to scare me?

Paul was not sure.

Who had been murdered?

All he knew was that he wasn't guilty. Then he thought about how he had acted. He ran from the cops and refused to talk to them.

Damn it, I made myself look guilty. Why? Why did I do that, to keep from squealing on my friends? I am such an idiot! They did not do anything wrong either. They didn't kill anyone. Shit, why did we even run? Oh yeah, we were carrying weapons. Crap!

Paul began adding up all the evidence against him in his head. He began leaning on all of the Law and Order episodes he had watched over the years and wondered if he should lawyer up. Second-guessing himself, he wondered if requesting an attorney would make him look guiltier.

Chapter 94

Malcolm awoke to the light of the morning. He instantly took a look at the hanging meat. The remains of the chipmunk were gone.

"Dang it!"

The snare had gone off, but failed to capture the coyote. He got his meat and undoubtedly would be back for more.

He hated to leave his spot. He became quite comfortable in the little tree well, but he knew that the coyote would return. Next time, he might have a few buddies to help him.

So with trepidation, Malcolm packed up his things and continued moving south.

He traveled along a small pond that was frozen over. The pond was the result of a hollowed section of granite. Other than a few tall trees, the pond was surrounded by rock.

Malcolm stopped and referred to his map. He found a lake that he was convinced was a similar shape to the one he stood next to. Without the ability to see the mountain ranges around him, he had nothing to triangulate with to confirm his position.

He tried to break through the ice to obtain fresh water, but the ice was too thick. Frustrated, he moved on.

With everything snowed over, it was impossible to locate any of the trails. Malcolm was discouraged with the thought of walking right over a trail without even knowing it. He knew he could literally be passing his 'road to salvation.'

He now realized the foolishness of his ways. How had he convinced himself that he could survive out here? Why hadn't he considered the fierce winters?

Actually, I thought I'd be dead by now.

He continued southwest. He traversed snow covered boulder fields, and scrambled down scree. He came upon a large snow bridge.

He knew the dangers of snow bridge crossings. There was a significant risk of breaking through and falling into a watery grave. Crossing alone increased the dangers of dying. At least with another person, there was a slim chance that they could react quickly, throwing a rescue line and pulling you out. Better yet, with a partner, he would insist on being tethered while crossing the terrain.

He thought back over the terrain he had just traversed. To travel back required scrambling back up the scree. That would burn all his strength, and he wasn't sure that it was even doable. He was in between a sheer rock cliff and the ravine that he wished to cross.

He examined the snow bridge, trying to guess at the thickness. It was impossible. There was no telling how much was solid ice versus loose snow on top. The bridge was wide enough to drive a Honda Civic across, but that didn't attest to the thickness in the middle.

Malcolm took his walking stick and performed a test probe of the bridge. The stick easily passed 6 inches through the powdery snow before stopping abruptly against the solid ice. Malcolm estimated the bridge to appear to be two to three feet thick, but one could never be completely sure.

With no real alternative, Malcolm took a few steps out onto the bridge. He listened intently for any sounds of cracking. He loosened the straps on his backpack and released the hip straps as a precaution.

Before each step, he used his pole to probe the bridge. Poised like a cat to spring back at any sign of a problem, he inched forward.

At what he estimated to be the halfway point, he shifted his focus to the other side of the ravine. His palms were sweating and his legs shook when he made the mistake of looking down the ravine. Should the ice give way or he slip, he would meet his demise by falling down the 60-foot waterfall.

"This is so sketchy," he repeated to himself.

I really should have crampons and a rope for this. Actually, I really should not be doing this.

Malcolm began to relax with three-quarters of the bridge crossing behind him. He began taking longer steps, and used his pole more for stability than probing.

Because of the uniform blanketing of the snow, it was impossible to know where the bridge ended and the solid ground began.

Malcolm climbed up the steep incline on the other side and stopped to catch his breath. His nerves were shot.

Chapter 95

"Kyle, you guys are in deep water right now. We just charged your friend with a number of charges; he's likely to go away for a very long time. Especially if the murder charges stick..."

"MURDER CHARGES!?!," Kyle interrupted. "What murder charges, we did not murder anybody."

"As I was saying, your friend could go away for a very long time. You on the other hand, you could help yourself. You still have an opportunity to cooperate. Your friend refused to tell us everything we wanted to know; that made matters worse for him. You have the upper hand here. So far, you have done the right thing. You did not run, did not resist arrest, and did not assault an officer," Stevenson reasoned.

Stevenson laid out the argument perfectly and had Kyle considering his options. Kyle wondered if this was all true or if the cops were bullshitting him in attempts to get him to rat on his friends.

"Honestly, Kyle, if you cooperate and you are innocent, you could be out of here in about an hour. If you dick around with us… well, we are likely to slap the same charges on you as we have done with your buddy there. So what do you say?"

Stevenson sat there in silence and watched as the cogs in Kyle's brain turned at high speed.

He loved using the tactic of silence. People become extremely uncomfortable in interviews and interrogations when the main guy doesn't say anything. They immediately begin thinking that something is wrong. More times than not, the person ends up spilling their guts and saying more than perhaps they ought.

Kyle thought it over briefly but still was not sure what to do. He waited for them to ask a question.

"Alright Kyle, here's the deal. You are only 17; you are still a minor, as far as we know you haven't done anything wrong. So either you start talking or we are going to be forced to play hard ball, beginning with charging you for obstruction of justice."

Kyle began blurting out, " we didn't do anything wrong. All we wanted to do was find the guy who has been kidnapping and killing our pets. What is so wrong with that? The guy took my dog, Mars. I've had that dog since I was 10 years old. It isn't right and you guys are too busy, or whatever, to do anything about it. We didn't hurt nobody, never found anything, and then all of a sudden you guys scare the shit out of us with a helicopter, flashing lights, and loud speakers. What did you expect us to do?"

Stevenson and Millard exchanged looks that let each other know that what the kid was saying sounded legit and believable.

"Alright, well, I'm sorry to hear about your dog, son, really, I am. I have a dog. I am crazy about him. I am scared about this guy stealing him too. Finding the guy responsible for all this is the department's top priority right now. I promise you that. Come on, most of the cops on the force have dogs and we have 20 K9 units. Think about it, you honestly think that we don't care?"

What Stevenson was saying made sense to Kyle.

"Listen, if you can tell us everything you know, then we can use the information to catch the SOB. Do you want to be part of the solution or part of the problem?"

Kyle conceded, "Ok, I understand. What do you want to know?"

Chapter 96

Stevenson thought about where to begin. He knew he had to handle Kyle with kid gloves. He didn't want to frighten him; that could shut him up. He had to gain Kyle's confidence. He wanted to make him feel that they were on his side and wanted to help.

"First off, being that you are a minor, we need to contact your parents. So far we haven't been able to reach them."

"They went up to the Sierra's with some friends, they are camping," Kyle offered.

Stevenson and Millard looked at each other and then the one-way mirror. Without parental consent or legal representation, they risked coercion of a minor. If he ended up confessing to something, it would be instantly thrown out.

"Go ahead, continue," the Sheriff's deep baritone voice ordered from the speaker.

"Ok, tell me when your dog... Mars, was it?"

Kyle nodded.

"Tell me when Mars went missing and any details about it."

Stevenson wanted Kyle to feel confident that they wanted to help him.

"Mars went missing a week ago."

"How do you know he was taken?"

"Well, he use to get out a lot, but he always found his way home. Everyone in the neighborhood knew him. But, he hasn't tried to get out for a long time. My Dad says it's because he's been getting older or more mature. Anyway, there are no signs of digging or busted fence boards or anything. The other thing is that I keep his leash on the patio table, and it is gone."

Stevenson was writing down notes, attempting to convey that he took Kyle's situation seriously.

"Ok, we are going to have you file a report for your dog, after we are finished here. We have a team dedicated to this. Now, I need some further information about what happened tonight, ok?"

Kyle nodded. Though none of the neighborhood liked cops, he had to admit that this guy was pretty cool.

"Kyle, I know that you want to be cool and protect your friends, but like you, if they didn't do anything wrong, they have no reason to worry. We need to clear their names from being suspect in stealing these pets. Can you tell me who was in your group tonight?"

Kyle worried about squealing. The officer was being real nice. If he gave up the names he would never live it down. Stevenson could see that he was having trouble with this.

"Alright Kyle, tell me this, how many were in your group? Can you tell me that much?"

"Five, there were five of us."

"Good, that's what we thought. Now, are they all from your neighborhood?"

"Yes," Kyle offered hesitantly.

"Are you the youngest in the group?"

"Yes."

"How did you get involved in this?"

"The guys knew my dog had been taken and they asked if I wanted to do something about it."

"Has everyone in the group had a pet go missing?"

"No, just me and Nick. But I've heard that lots of pets have been missing all over the place. And the guys said that's all that anyone is talking about down at Raliegh's."

Stevenson did not react to the name being leaked, but he was hoping that the guys on the other side of the glass were acting on it. Kyle mentioned Raliegh's, he knew the Pub well. Perhaps the other guys were regulars and they could pick up a lead there.

"So the rest of the guys, they were just trying to help, including Paul?"

"Yes, they just wanted to find the guy and stop him. Honest. We were going to get the guy."

"And what, then call us?"

"Um, yea, I don't know. It just isn't right, and we were trying to help."

"I understand. Listen, we can't just let you go. We have to release you to a responsible adult. If your parents can't be reached, is there somebody else? A relative, maybe?"

"Yeah, my Uncle. Uncle Steve. He'll come down and get me."

"Great, we'll have somebody contact him to come get you."

Tapping on the glass interrupted their conversation. The door opened and somebody on the outside whispered to Millard. Stevenson and Kyle sat there waiting to find out what was going on.

Millard opened the door and stood to the side to allow a woman in uniform enter.

Millard explained, "Kyle, we need to get a dental impression from you. This will give us proof of your innocence and allow us to drop all charges and let you go. Will that be alright with you?"

"What? Um, what does my teeth have to do with missing pets? I don't understand," Kyle responded.

He genuinely looked confused. Stevenson felt for the kid.

"Listen, we can't give you details about the case, but we do have a warrant to obtain either your impressions or your dental records. Either way, we are going to obtain your bite mark. You will be saving both of us a lot of time if you just willingly provide it here and now. Otherwise, we will locate your dentist and get your records. That could take a day or two and you'd be waiting in the cell until we could clear you. It's up to you, man."

Kyle still did not understand why they needed his dental impressions, but he conceded. It wasn't bad at all, they just had him bite down on a couple of thin pieces of tin foil like strips.

"Ok, we are done here. I'm just going to give you one last chance to share with us the names of the others in your group."

Stevenson thought he'd give it one last try, though he pretty much knew Kyle would not divulge the information.

"I'm sorry, really I am, but I can't. I can't tell you."

"Alright. Well, while they process your impressions, let's get you over to draw up the report on your missing dog. Your Uncle should be here any minute."

Chapter 97

After the bridge crossing, Malcolm did not dare sit down because the bank was a sheet of hardened ice. The southern exposure caused the ice to melt and then freeze again each night. This caused a slick hardened surface that was also prone for an avalanche.

Malcolm wanted to quickly make his way off of the sheet of ice. He turned around, facing the ice, he kicked his toes into the ice, making small steps as he made his way down the sheet of ice. Each step was a scary unknown. He was risking causing the sheet to break loose and slide with him on it. His only alternative was to risk slipping off the ice and into the ravine below.

He finally made it down to a solid outcropping of rock. He took a minute to regain his composure and to examine his next venture.

He looked down off the cropping from which he stood. There was a 30-foot section of loose scree that ended on a 3-foot wide ledge. Beyond that, was a severe drop, down the ravine to the bottom of the frozen waterfall.

Malcolm made the diehard decision to lower his backpack down to the ledge. He feared that the added weight on his back would cause him to be top heavy and likely push him over the ledge. He hated parting with all of his gear.

If I lose my gear?

He refused to think of what might come of him.

With a couple of deep encouraging breaths, Malcolm began surfing down the scree. He firmly placed his feet on the ledge and grabbed a root sticking out of the dirt. The root broke free. Malcolm lunged onto a boulder, hugging the natural life preserver.

After regaining his composure, he located his backpack, and easily traversed the snow-covered granite. He followed the frozen stream, watching the snakelike form make its way to the meadows below. He walked along the stream, continually running through his mind, the events that he just experienced. He felt fortunate to still be alive.

Chapter 98

"Stevenson, Millard, can I see you guys in my office," the Sheriff bellowed out.

The two officers made their way into the office. Millard closed the door behind him as he entered.

The Sheriff began, "Ok, so the kid is innocent, and it sounds like the group was a bunch of boys trying to be vigilante heroes. I do not want to assume anything here. We need to find the rest of the group and clear them from suspicion. I don't want this being one of those crazy cases where we had a lead and the perp passed right below our noses. So how are we going to find out who these boys are?"

Millard jumped first, "Kyle dropped the name Nick. Said he was missing his dog as well. We can check to see if a Nick called in about a missing dog and find out who he is that way. He also said that the rest of the gang hanged out at Raliegh's. We could head down there and ask around."

The Sheriff interjected, "I sent a couple guys out to Raliegh's as soon as I heard the kid say that. They talked to the bartender who wasn't much help at all. We are not going to get much cooperation out of the neighborhood. The missing dog report will be a long shot, but give it 5 minutes of your time, no more. After the Uncle comes and picks up the kid, let's get Paul back in here and lean on him some more. You could make it sound like Kyle ratted on him."

"Have they got impressions from Paul," Stevenson asked?

"No, not yet. Why don't you guys go and help them with that and then drag him out here in cuffs. Let him see Kyle going free before questioning him further."

"Sounds good, we're on it," Millard stated as they rose and left the office.

Chapter 99

As Millard and Stevenson left the Sheriff's office, they saw Kyle's Uncle arrive. His face was a contorted mix of worried and peeved. When his eyes finally located Kyle, he ran up to him.

As he approached he told him, "Don't say anything. Keep your mouth shut."

Millard took this one, "s'cuse me, are you Steve, Kyle's Uncle?"

"Yes, yes I am. What did he do?"

"Well, we are waiting for the results of a test we are running, but as of now we have nothing. Kyle appears to be innocent and we'll be releasing him to your care." Millard informed Steve. "It appears that Kyle was merely hanging out with the wrong group of guys."

"What? Who? What guys, what did they do?"

Steve seemed genuinely concerned.

"Well, Sir, as for what they did, we have charged one of the guys with assaulting an officer, resisting arrest, and possibly murder. As far as who, well Kyle has refused to share with us the names of the rest of his gang."

"Gang? What? Kyle is not part of a gang." Steve turned his attention to Kyle.

"Kyle, what are they talking about? What have you gotten yourself into? You listen and you listen good, you tell them the names of those guys right now. These are serious charges and you do not want to be part of this, do you understand?"

Kyle tried to ignore his Uncle.

Steve raised his voice, "Was it Brian, Paul, or Gregory? No, it was probably Nick and Dillon? Or was it Sanchez and his boys? Who was it? You weren't messin around with Koreem again?

"I'm serious, listen to me. This is one of those moments that we've talked about. One of those defining moments that will end up affecting the rest of your life. You need to think long and hard about what the right thing to do here is going to be," Steve attempted to counsel.

Steve addressed the Deputies, "How many guys were there and what did they look like?"

Stevenson was busy writing down every name that came out of Steve's mouth.

Millard answered, "We have Paul in a jail cell right now. There were 5 guys total, but we only managed to apprehend Kyle and Paul. The only other name we've managed to obtain is a Nick, but we haven't had any luck figuring out who he is."

Steve offered, "Nick? Nick's last name is Mathson. Most of the neighborhood just calls him Mathson. He lives on Saratoga. If

Paul and Mathson were involved, I'd put my money on Dillon being involved as well."

Steve noticed Kyle's gaze drop to the floor and his head lowered, he knew he was on target.

Steve continued, "And if Dillon was involved, his older brother Gregory would have been there just for fun. Am I missing anybody Kyle?"

Kyle refused to acknowledge his Uncle. Steve swatted Kyle's head making a loud slapping sound that made everyone flinch.

"Kyle, am I missing anyone," Steve repeated.

Kyle slowly shook his head.

"There you go officers. Whatever you need, we will fully cooperate, won't we Kyle?"

Steve grabbed a fistful of Kyle's hair and forced him to nod in compliance.

"Great, do you have last names of these guys, addresses, or know where we can find them?"

Steve looked at them, wondered if he should just offer to do their jobs for them, and then asked for a piece of paper. He drew a crude map of the neighborhood and marked the homes where each of the guys lived.

"I don't know the house numbers, but you should be able to figure it out from this map. And fellas, if it comes down to it, you didn't get the information from us."

"Mums the word," Stevenson promised.

"Alright, are we free to take off now," Steve asked.

"One second, let me check on the test results."

Millard picked up his phone and called down to forensics.

"Did we get a match on the bites? Are you sure? Cause I'm about to let the kid go. Ok then, thanks."

"Alright, looks like you are free to go."

Just as Kyle was standing to leave, Paul was being escorted to the interrogation room. Their eyes met.

Chapter 100

Malcolm was forced to skirt around the large meadow. The tall reeds and swampy soil made it difficult to navigate. Additionally, the snow acted as a blanket, disguising dangerous pitfalls.

Traveling clockwise, he made his way around the meadow. He was forced to cross several small streams, most of which were dried and none of which were larger than the one he had been following.

After several hours, Malcolm made it to the other end of the meadow. He located the outflow of all the water. Having joined several other sources of water, the stream had more than doubled in size.

Malcolm's heart skipped a beat when his eyes located what looked to be a path on the other side of the river. He stood still, attempting to scan the trail in either direction. He imagined the form of the trail and how it would look in the absence of snow.

Pulling out the map, Malcolm tried to determine his location. By his calculations, he was either in or near the Yosemite National

Park border. The cloud cover and dense forest made it impossible to pinpoint his location with any certainty.

The meadow and river that he located on his map did not indicate a trail following the river. Despite the difference between what he saw and what was on the map, Malcolm made the decision to follow the trail.

Not wanting to risk becoming wet in these conditions, he skirted along the opposite side of the river from the trail. Periodically, he would glance across to confirm that the flat indentation in the snow bank continued.

Malcolm came to a steep embankment and was forced to crawl up and over a mound of snow. As he crested the mound, he heard what sounded like muffled pops. He wondered if the sound was gunfire from far away. Before he could finish the thought, the ground below him gave way.

The ground dropped out from beneath his feet and Malcolm found himself riding a sheet of snow-covered ice toward the icy waters 20 feet below.

Acting on instinct and adrenaline, Malcolm hurled his body off of the sliding ice and onto a large boulder that he had not consciously known was there. He landed on his feet but instantly dropped on his belly and bear-hugged the rock.

He turned his head and watched as the sheet of ice submerged and then floated down the river, breaking into pieces each time it bumped into a rock.

Malcolm sat up on the rock that had saved his life. He took stock in his surroundings. He found irony in the fact that the rock that saved his life now had him stranded in the middle of a deadly river.

"Isn't it ironic? Don't you think?" His tribute to Alanis Morissette.

Chapter 101

Paul saw Kyle standing with his Uncle Steve at one of the officer's desk. He wondered what was going on. The cops pushed him into the room before he could figure it out.

He sat in there for a period of time until he began wondering if they had forgot about him. As he stood to find out what happened to everyone, the door burst open.

"Sit. We have some things to discuss. First things first, we are going to take a bite impression of your teeth."

"What?"

"We are going to take a bite impression of your teeth. It will tell us if you did or did not commit the murders."

"This is crazy, what murders? Ask Kyle, we didn't kill anybody," Paul argued.

"We did ask Kyle, he refused to talk. He did, however, give us his bite impressions and he is now on his way home. So what do you say?"

"Do I have to? Do you have a warrant?"

Stevenson slammed the court order on top of the table with a loud bang. There was no reason for Paul to be putting up such a fuss.

Without reading the order Paul asked, "If I do this, will you let me go?"

"Depends on the results of the test."

"Right, of course, but then will you let me go?"

"We are going to get your bite marks one way or another. You have no chips to bargain with here. You still have other charges that you need to answer to. It is looking like you'll be staying the night so the department can figure out what to do with you. Maybe a night in the slammer will help adjust your poor attitude."

Paul ignored the condescending cheap shot. Instead he nodded his head to show his compliance with the test. Millard opened the door and a woman walked in and performed the quick test.

After the test was finished, Millard replaced the handcuffs on Paul and they escorted him back to the cell.

Chapter 102

Paul was placed in the cell and was surprised to find Gregory and Nick.

"What are you guys doing here? I thought you got away," Paul inquired.

Nick replied, "we did. We all met back at Raliegh's. Then a couple cops stopped by there looking for us. So then we decided to head home. We went to Dillon's and tried to think of what to do next. We didn't know if they got you or what."

"Ok, so then what happened," Paul encouraged.

"Well, we were there for a couple of hours, then all these cops showed up," Gregory said with an accusatory look and tone.

"Knock it off, I haven't told them anything. Why do you think I'm still in here and Kyle's out free?"

"What, they let Kyle go, " Gregory asked. "I knew having the kid around would bite us in the ass."

"Kyle wouldn't do that and you both know it. They must have asked around or something. Who knows, they got us and that's what matters now," Nick reasoned.

"Hey, where's Dillon," Paul asked.

"Oh, they took him for questioning, right after they made us all bite some tinfoil crap."

"Yeah, me too. Has something to do with some murders they are trying to pin on us."

"Murders!?!" Gregory and Nick said in unison. "What murders?"

"No idea, they haven't said more than that. It's bogus, they are just trying to scare us."

Chapter 103

Malcolm mentally went through his belongings. He tried to think of anything that he had that could help him get from the boulder to shore. The river was not flowing too fast to prevent him from forging; it was just the threat of hypothermia.

Between him and where he had come from were a deep pool and a steep embankment. The other direction appeared to be waste deep and a gradual embankment.

I guess there is no decision to be made on which shore to go for. Apparently the man upstairs is guiding me, Malcolm thought as he turned his eyes heavenward.

As he offered his combined prayer of gratitude and request for help, he noticed that the skies were growing dark. He had no idea what time of day it was, but it appeared to be nearing evening. He had to do something quick. Inaction would leave him exposed to the elements and without a doubt he would die on this rock.

Knowing that he could not risk his clothes or boots getting wet, he stripped down and carefully placed everything into his backpack.

Before lowering himself off of the rock, Malcolm examined the shoreline. He mentally recorded locations where firewood and kindling could be found. He chose a location to build a fire and secured his flashlight on top of his load for quick access.

Completely nude and exposed, he rolled over onto his belly. The rock quickly sucked out warmth from his naked body. He instantly began shivering as he slid his body down the side of the boulder. The rough texture of the boulder grabbed at his pale goose-bumped skin.

Reaching out for purchase, his toes touched the icy waters and instinctually pulled back. Malcolm felt his chest seize in anticipation of the freezing waters. It became difficult to breath as he forced his feet into the water. His feet came to rest just inches into the waters and Malcolm felt a strange relief as he pushed his body away from the rocky cold mass.

He reached out his left foot and searched for solid footing. Slowly and methodically, he crossed the river. His feet ached with coldness. The freezing waters were actually painful. He expected the numbness, but the pain was beyond anything he anticipated.

The numbness of the cold was not enough to protect his feet from agony as he stepped on sharp rocks and stubbed his toes in search of each footing. He was extremely careful with each step; to slip now would be detrimental.

Malcolm raised his eyes upstream and caught a glimpse of the enormous mountain that he had descended. He wondered how he could possibly still be alive. He continued moving.

Each gasp for air turned into a screech of pain. He did not recognize the voice that was exiting his mouth. The voice sounded foreign, high pitched, and wild.

As he neared the shoreline, the depth suddenly dropped.

Malcolm found himself whimpering as the waters quickly rose to hip level. His feet were so numb, that the granite rocks and pebbles now felt like mud.

Chapter 104

Sheriff Glasgow was unable to keep up with the amount of activity that was happening. The crowd outside was continuing to grow and all his officers were constantly stopping people on the streets. He called a meeting of his section chiefs to gather a perspective on their efforts.

"Ok guys, we have been working on this all night. From what I understand, we have a number of people in our cells. We are booked to capacity and are not able to keep up with the processing. Conner, can you give us an update on operations?"

Conner was the deputy assigned as Section Chief of Operations. He stepped to the front of the room to address everyone.

"Well, as the Sheriff stated, we have been at this all night. Our guys are exhausted and we need to rotate shifts to give adequate breaks. Through the efforts of our operation, we have arrested a number of people from all over the county. We have been comparing impressions with bite marks. So far, we do not have any matches. We need more trained personnel to process all the impressions. Unless we have another reason for keeping them, we have been releasing people as soon as their impressions do not match. That's all I have for now."

The Sheriff stood and thanked Deputy Conner. "Ok, Plans is Roper."

Deputy Roper rose and walked to the front of the room.

"The plan continues as is. We have covered the densely populated areas of the county. Today, the plan is to spread out into the rural areas. We have a major backlog of debriefings that need to be incorporated into plans; this could take a couple of days. We haven't been able to upload the GPS tracks from last night, currently this is our biggest hurdle."

"What is going on with the GPS tracks," the Sheriff asked.

"From what I understand, the system was overloaded and logistics is working on it," Roper said with a shoulder shrug.

"Ok, anything that you need," the Sheriff inquired.

"Besides triple the man power? Yeah. We were thinking that it would be good to call in our Search and Rescue volunteers to provide relief and assistance. Also, we would like to ask the rangers of the regions parks and open space to search and report on their areas. Not sure if it is appropriate to ask for mutual aid from State, but we could use the help. Finally, we would suggest involving further involvement of the public."

"Duly noted, Logistics, did you get all that," Sheriff asked.

"Yes, Sir. Got it," Kevin responded.

The Sheriff responded to Roper's report.

"Roper, I know this is stressful, but all we have, is all we have at the moment. We cannot request mutual aid, because as I understand it, this problem is wide spread. I've made contact with neighboring counties, and they are reporting similar problems. I like the idea of contacting regional parks. As far as further involvement of the public, we'll address this in a moment.

"Ok, Kevin you are a go with logistics."

"Thanks Sheriff Glasgow. Ok, we have every conceivable vehicle in deployment, including many personal vehicles. All three helicopters have been in the sky above the county. We have asked for Highway Patrol to provide additional eyes in the sky, but they are overwhelmed at the moment. Our radios are all on their backup batteries and will only be available until those run dead. We are charging the batteries as they come in, but we are now sending teams out without handhelds. We have been forced to use personal mobile phones for primary communications. Again, this is only reliable for as long as the phones can remain charged. Most of our guys do not carry chargers for their phones. We do have coffee, doughnuts, and pastries for teams as they come in for rehab. And, we are in the process of organizing lunches."

"What is going on with the GPS uploading?"

"We typically upload the GPS tracks of a few units at a time. The system is not fast enough to process all the tracks that have been coming in. The system overloaded last night around 3 and we've been playing catch up ever since," Kevin informed.

"Ok, thanks Kevin. All right, so where we stand, I think it would be best to scale back out efforts for the day. All of these attacks appear to be happening during the night hours, so I want to scale back for the day, focus on processing the data we have gathered, and we'll go from there. Good work everybody."

"So are we doing it again tonight," Roper yelled out.

"From what I hear, it is unlikely that we will have all the data processed by then. So, tell everyone to remain available, but most likely, we'll resume tomorrow night. This will give everyone some time to recoup," the Sheriff informed.

"What's going on with the press release," Conner asked.

"Press Representative Sam Carquinez has been the main contact for the press. He delivered two releases throughout the night and is scheduled to deliver information at 0900 this morning. Because we do not have anything solid, we have been telling the public to be careful and remain indoors at night. Any other questions?"

With no further questions presented, the Sheriff ended the briefing and sent everyone on their way.

Roper approached him privately.

"Sir, have you heard any response from the FBI?"

"No, I do not know what is going on, but I am not liking it one bit."

"Yeah, this is looking widespread and scary."

"I know, don't worry too much about it though. We take care of our own."

Roper shook his head and walked away.

Chapter 105

The Sheriff walked back to his office, closed the door, and with a heavy exhalation – sat down behind his desk. He had his arms raised and perched on his head with his fingers interlaced. He tried to think of what should occur next. He had exhausted his resources and came up short. He considered the facts that were known so far. He learned that this was not a problem confined to his county. He now new that they were not dealing with a mountain lion, but a group of people – probably a cult of some sort. He wasn't sure what the range was, but at least 3 counties wide. And he learned that they were killing people as well as animals.

What is going on, he wondered.

There was a knock on the door.

So much for peace and quiet.

"Yeah, come in," the Sheriff bellowed.

Sam Carquinez entered the room.

"Sheriff, I am preparing the 0900 statement for the press, is there anything specific that you would like me to incorporate?"

"I don't know, 'Get your affairs in order cause all hell is breaking loose."

"Yeah, I know. This is bizarre and crazy shit we're dealing with. Any idea how far this group has gone? Maybe they are traveling," Sam offered.

The Sheriff paused for a brief second, considering what Sam had offered.

"Sheriff? You ok? I could come back."

"No, sorry. I'm all yours. Why don't you read to me what you have so far?"

"Sure;
> Over the past few days, our community has been plagued by a group of felons who have allegedly stolen several pets and apparently been consuming them. The thefts have occurred at night. The Sheriff's office has been maximizing efforts to catch the members of this gang. We do not know how many people are in this gang, nor do we have any witnesses or descriptions. The department is strongly suggesting that everyone stay inside, behind locked doors, with their pets for the time being. Any and all suspicious activity should be reported immediately. There has been a number of vigilante activity around the county. The Sheriff's department is asking the community to please be patient and cease this activity. It is forcing the department to waste valuable time and resources. Last night the department became bogged down in

dealing with vigilant activity. This pulls resources away from the task at hand and does more harm than good. The extent of your vigilant duty involves reporting any questionable activity or individuals that you see. Again, please stay indoors at night, for the time being.

"Yes, it sounds good. It sums things up without divulging too much. I think you aptly got the point across that these vigilantes are doing more harm than good. Who knows, we may have caught the guys last night if we weren't forced to chase these do-gooders around."

"Ok, and you still think that it is a good idea to not share information about the murders?"

"I want to wait a little bit longer, until we know what we are dealing with. You see how people react when just pets are involved; can you imagine what could happen if they knew their loved ones were at risk?"

Chapter 106

Reaching the bank, Malcolm pulled himself out of the river. Strangely, the snow was a relief and felt warmer to him. His body was shivering uncontrollably.

He quickly set about drying off and dressing. He had severe difficulty pulling his clothes over the numb stubs that were once his feet. After he finished dressing, Malcolm took his stuff over to the location he had made a visual scouting of.

He placed his bag down and fired up his Jet Boil. The fire sputtered and died.

"SHIT! SHIT! SHIT!"

Malcolm had been rationing his fuel the whole time he had been in the wilderness. Now, when he needed it most, the fuel ran out.

What a perfect time for this to happen.

He was frustrated and threw the Jet Boil against a tree. The clank of the metal against the tree was anticlimactic, frustrating him even more.

Ok, you're hypothermic. You are agitated, you're shivering uncontrollably. I have to get warm. PUSH UPS!

He dropped to the ground and performed 13 pushups before collapsing.

Get up! Get up! Get up, you loser!

Malcolm laid there. He began wondering how long it would take to fall asleep. He could just close his eyes and he'd certainly be dead within a couple of hours.

I could think of worse ways to go.

Fire! Get the fire going. Come on, you are not a quitter, don't quit now. Get up and get a fire going.

He forced himself up onto his knees. He looked around and tried to make sense of where he had decided to gather wood and kindling. He stood up and began stumbling toward the fallen trees.

Breaking off bark from the dead tree, Malcolm gathered the sawdust into his hands. He took it back to his clearing and began building the fire. First spreading a layer of sawdust and pine needles, then he built a teepee with the chunks of bark he had gathered.

Malcolm broke off a fist-sized ball of sap that clung to the side of a pine tree. He took the sticky sap and placed it under the teepee structure he had built.

He bent down and with his flashlight, he lit a small pile of shavings and pine needles. He held the pile in his palms and gently blew on the sparks. The sparks ignited the material and burst into a smoldering flame. He continued to supply oxygen as he carefully transplanted the bundle beneath the teepee.

The pine needles and sawdust struggled to ignite. The ball of sap spat as the water content defrosted. Soon the sap ignited and exhausted a blue flame that quickly engulfed the ball.

The flame warmed his nose and cheeks. He begged the warmth to spread throughout his body and offer him relief. The warmth only served as a reminder of how cold he truly was.

He continued to breath life into his fire. The flame spread and began burning the miniature teepee. His spirit rose with the smoke as he began adding wood to the growing flame.

Chapter 107

The Sheriff was just about to check his messages when his door flew open, banged against the wall, and Roper hastily entered with a paper in his hand.

"Sheriff, you'll want to read this. Just received this on the fax machine from the FBI."

FBI BOLO

Attention all law enforcement agencies. The FBI has received an unprecedented amount of calls requesting assistance. All resources have been deployed at this time. The BOLO system has been employed as the quickest and most efficient means for contacting all law enforcement agencies.

We are experiencing a nationwide pandemic of crime. The crimes involve kidnapping, mutilating, killing, and the consumption of humans and animals.

Little is known about the current events. We do not

know who is behind this, why they are doing it, or how to stop them.

Be On the Look Out for any groups or individuals acting erratically. Encourage communities to report any suspicious activities.

Further information will be provided as it becomes available.

"Holy Shit! This problem just keeps growing. Ok, let's contact state and local authorities and find out about enacting a mandatory curfew."

"You got it."

Chapter 108

Dr. Blythe Aspen was exhausted. She had been at the office and on duty for 72 hours straight. Her back ached from taking power naps at her desk. She was so tired that the coffees and power drinks no longer had any affect. She knew her body needed sleep and felt her bed calling out to her. It was 11:00am, typically a slow period for arriving bodies, as good as any a time to escape.

The office was full of personnel, all of who were concerned for her health and well-being. Blythe was one who always maintained her composure and appearance. She was now into her second day of not showering. By the third day, she gave up on reapplying her makeup. This added to the worries of her colleagues, and they urged her to go home.

As Blythe drove herself home, she contemplated staying at a hotel instead. She knew that her neighbors would be playing loud music, have friends over, slamming doors for no apparent reason, and smoking up a storm. She cursed her former neighbors for moving out and selling the place to young girls.

To mask the sounds from downstairs, Blythe had tried everything.

She left the TV on, she purchased a sound machine to create white noise during her slumber, and she tried to where earplugs – but they bugged her too much.

As she turned onto her street, she prayed that they wouldn't be there, that they were both working or better yet, on an extended vacation. Briefly, she hoped that the serial killer(s) had gotten them and eaten them alive. She smiled at the morbid thought, then quickly shook the thought out of her head. She felt remorseful for even allowing her thoughts to go that far – *even if the girls deserved a slow and painful death.*

Blythe pulled her Mercedes into her parking spot in front of her garage. She waited for the door to finish opening. She frowned when she saw the neighbor's car sitting in their driveway.

Maybe staying in a hotel was the way to go.

She pulled her car forward into the garage, slowly and carefully to compensate for fatigue, turned off the ignition, and pressed the remote to close the door. She sat there in the soft glow of the light illuminating from the garage door opener. After the machine stopped running, there was finally quiet.

Blythe sat there in the driver's seat of her car, soaking in the quiet. She relished in the soft cushioned leather and how it perfectly molded her body. She closed her eyes for just a second to enjoy the peaceful surroundings.

Chapter 109

Malcolm allowed himself the chance to relax as his face, hands, and feet thawed. The warmth of the fire was the best feeling Malcolm could ever recall experiencing.

He sat there, aware that the night had set in, but not really caring. He had built a respectable fire. It had quickly melted a ten-foot circumference in the snow directly around the fire. Malcolm spent the effort to dig a channel and divert the melted snow away from the fire. He collected as much of the water as he could.

He placed all of his containers near the fire and continually drank the warmed water. The shivering had long since subsided, but he still felt chilled to the bone. He warmed himself from the inside with warm water.

He contemplated sleeping out under the stars, next to the fire, but thought better of it. As soon as his fingers were nimble enough, he set about creating his shelter for the night.

He used what was left of his tent to create a barrier from the wet ground. He then propped up the rainfly with his broken tent poles to create a lean-to. He prayed that the winds would not blow this night. He anchored the fly as best he could with snow, bungee cord, and rocks.

The lean-to instantly reflected heat from the fire and he wondered why he hadn't thought of this previously.

After adding more wood to the fire, Malcolm climbed into his sleeping bag and fell asleep, while gnawing on a strip of dried rabbit.

Chapter 110

Dr. Aspen jumped awake to the buzzing and loud ringing of her phone. Not ringing exactly, she had downloaded a ring tone specifically for work. The phone sang out with the tone of "Another One Bites the Dust," by the British rock band Queen.

She grabbed the phone that was dancing around on the dashboard.

"Aspen."

"Hey Doc, hadn't heard from you and wanted to make sure you made it home safely," Trish's bubbly voice rang out.

"Oh, yes, um, yes, I am home. Everything is good. Thanks for calling," Blythe responded.

"Ok then, get some rest."

"Right, ok, bye."

Blythe was thinking how annoyingly ironic it was that Trish woke her up to tell her to get some sleep. She wasn't sure how long she was out, but it felt good. She made an attempt to repeat the slumber, but could not convince her body to relax and return to the dream state.

With a deep sigh, she gathered her belongings and stepped out of the vehicle. She closed and locked the door to the garage and then made her way up the concrete steps to her condo.

As she climbed the steps she thought about how quiet it seemed and hoped that the girls had left while she was sleeping in her car.

She fumbled with her keys; holding the screen door with her hip and juggling her belongings. She got the door unlocked and pushed her way in. The stale smell of a closed up residence hit her square in the sinuses. She dropped her belongings on the floor, kicked off her heels, threw her keys on the table, then turned around to close and lock the front door.

Blythe could not stand the stale-musty air. She moved around the condo counter-clockwise, opening all the windows and turning on the ceiling fans.

When she got to the kitchen, she poured a glass of chilled chardonnay, grabbed an apple and a string-cheese, and went out onto her back balcony.

She sat, sipping her wine, and enjoyed the sunlight on her face. She loved her balcony. From here she had a view of the bay waters. She often sat out here to watch sailboats and tankers pass by. Though she was a dozen or so blocks away from the water, the hill she sat on afforded her fantastic views.

She hiked up her dress, up around her waste, so her thighs were exposed to the sunlight. Then she pulled her shoulders and arms out of the dress to prevent embarrassing tan-lines.

She took another sip of her wine, closed her eyes, leaned her head back, and took a deep breath. She nearly choked as she gagged on the smell. She risked taking another deep breath; again the putrid smell assaulted her.

The smell was unmistakable; she knew the smell well – too well. She was instantly mortified at the thought of the decomposing stench of those corpses clinging to her clothes. The faces of everyone she came across over the course of the previous three days ran through her mind.

She pulled up the fabric of her dress and cautiously sampled the scent. Not smelling anything remotely as offensive, she dared a deeper inhalation.

Ok, thank goodness it isn't my clothes.

Next she lifted her right arm and stuck her nose into her armpit. Finding relief, she sampled the left armpit and was greeted by the flowery scent of her anti-perspirant.

She moved her investigation onto her hair. While it did not smell great and was in desperate need of a shower; it was not the source of the scent of death.

She followed the scent and gazed over the edge of her balcony to the hillside below. Nothing.

She pulled back her outdoor rug and peered down through the cracks between the deck boards at her neighbors' balcony below.

She moved her head back and forth trying to get a good indication of what was down there. She dropped the rug when she saw her neighbor staring back at her.

Chapter 111

"Adrianne? Adrianne, are you down there?"

Blythe waited for a response and heard nothing from her neighbor down below.

"Adrianne, do you smell that horrible smell? Do you know what it is? It smells like something died."

Nothing.

"It smells like it is coming from your place. When was the last time you guys cleaned?"

She giggled to herself, waiting for an agitated response. She contemplated momentarily about her sick sense of humor.

"Honey, if you don't answer me, I am going to assume that you are dead and call the cops."

Blythe pulled the rug back and peered down again. She could see Adrianne sitting in her patio chair. She could see the remains of a cigarette in her fingers, long since burnt out.

Blythe tried to get a better view, straining over the balcony to gain a full view of her neighbor. She gave up and ran through her condo, down the stairs, and rang the bell of her pesky neighbors.

After several attempts of ringing and knocking, Blythe ran around the garages and down the side of the building. She slowly approached the banister of her neighbor's condo. She peeked her head around the corner.

Despite dealing with death day in and day out, Blythe could not help but scream when she saw her neighbor. Adrianne's body sat in her chair, cigarette in hand, and dried blood that had drained from her neck and down her left arm.

Strangely, there was not more than a small puddle of blood on the decking; less than a third of a pint. Blythe ducked her head under the decking to see how much of the blood had seeped through. Oddly enough, there was not enough to suggest that Adrianne had bled to death where she sat.

Blythe strained for a closer look at the site of the bleed. There was not any sign of bite marks. From where Blythe stood, it appeared as though her neck was sliced.

Suicide? But where is the knife and all the blood?

Chapter 112

The weather cooperated throughout the night. Malcolm only woke up once to add wood to the fire. The heat continued to emanate from the fire. Malcolm sucked his tongue, rubbing it against the inside of his mouth. Breathing the heat all night had dried out his throat. He reached over to his cup and quickly drained its content down his parched throat.

Having melted the snow and exposing the ground, the fire revealed the roots of the nearby trees. Malcolm set about digging out the smallest and easiest to chew roots of the pines. The pinecones were too high for him to reach, so he focused on the roots.

Even though he doubted any success of catching a fish, he baited his line and set up his rod near the river. Then he set about breaking camp and preparing for the hike.

After loading up his bag, Malcolm walked away from the stream to relieve himself. He crouched behind the fallen tree from which he had secured the fuel for his fire. As he crouched, he glanced around at his surroundings. His eyes stopped on a nearby tree.

The bark was all but stripped off the tree. He looked inquisitively at the tree, trying to make since of what he was looking at. He looked at another tree and began to decipher what he saw.

Bears! Crap!

He pulled up his pants, searched his surroundings, and quietly made his way back to his gear.

As he retraced his steps, he then noticed bear tracks in the snow, all around him.

He was so frazzled the night before; he failed to notice the signs of bear activity. He was nervous that they might appear at any moment.

Previously, he had hoped that the bears were all hibernating. Now he knew that this was not the case.

He quickly made his way back to the stream, grabbed his rod, and began hastily reeling in the line.

He met resistance and instantly thought to himself, "*If this line is caught, I'm just gonna cut it.*"

He continued to reel and realized that he had a fish on the end of his line.

No wonder the bears like it here.

He pulled the fish in hastily while glancing around. He was prepared to ditch the fish as soon as a bear showed up. He removed the knife from his side, flipped open the blade and lowered the fish onto a rock.

He poked the point of his knife into the belly of the fish, just above the anus. He slid the knife up effortlessly. Sliding his index finger into the throat of the fish, with a couple tugs, Malcolm removed all the innards and bones from the fish. He tossed the guts and skeletal remains into the river. Then he rinsed the fish, knife, and rock. Then he quickly ate the fish raw.

He could not risk hiking with the smell of fish. So he quickly ate the fish raw, and then washed his hands and face in the ice-cold river water.

He returned to his gear, hiked his bag onto his back and began hiking down the snow-covered trail.

Chapter 113

"OH, you have got to be kidding me!"

Malcolm had only hiked a fraction of a mile when the trail disappeared into the river before reappearing on the opposite side. He stood there staring at the cold river.

The last crossing nearly killed him. He wondered how many times this trail would end up crossing waterways. He considered abandoning the trail, but then thought better of the idea.

The river was shallow here, the obvious reason for the crossing location. He played out the crossing in his mind. If he got wet, he would have to make a fire on the other side and stay the night there. This translated into a whopping 1-mile progression from his previous camp.

The frustration boiled inside him. The angst would prevent Malcolm from making sound decisions. He sat down on the bank of the river and took a deep breath. He had no choice but to forge the river. He sat there staring at the passing water as if waiting for another option to come floating by.

Resolving to face the music of the situation, Malcolm stood on his feet and began to mentally prepare for the freezing and wet crossing. He glanced up the river and then down, willing for another option.

Just as he was bending down to remove his boots, he noticed a dark horizontal line in the river below him. He stood on a rock and squinted his eyes, trying to make since of the linear depiction in a world of the non-linear.

Not 50 yards from where he stood, was a tree crossing. A tree had been placed for hikers to cross the river, not uncommon in the Sierras. He had failed to notice the log-bridge because it was covered in snow and blended in with the riverbank further down stream. It was the dark underside of the log that had caught his eye.

Malcolm's spirit rose as he ran through the snowdrifts down to the crossing. The main crossing was obviously for horses and pack mules, where the log was there to help keep hikers dry. Malcolm was near singing in his elation level as he approached the log.

The log was covered in a foot of snow. Normally, the log would be an easy crossing. With the snow, the crossing became challenging. Still, it was far less challenging than stripping down and wading the frozen waters.

Malcolm loosened the straps on his backpack, and began carefully selecting his foot placement on the log. He continued moving across, one foot at a time. The river rushing five feet below, taunted him. Halfway across, Malcolm realized he was holding his breath. He let it out on the next step and took in a slow deep breath on the sequential foot placement.

He was three-quarters of the way across, when his foot slipped off the edge of the log. Immediately, he fell to his belly and bear hugged the bridge. His legs dangled off the edge and he could hear the snow and ice splash into the river. He kicked his legs, searching for momentum to aid in regaining his position on the log.

He pulled with his arms, but the buckle on his waistband dug into the bark preventing him from raising himself. He continued fighting the caught buckle, but to no avail. Fatigue was setting in fast. He swung his left leg up onto the log and caught his heal. He strong-legged the log and pivoted his hips out and up onto the log. His arms began shaking as he struggled to pull himself to safety.

Malcolm took a deep breath and then grunted while he made the attempt to haul the rest of his body onto the top of the crossing. His heel came loose. His legs swung beneath him with so much force that his fingers could not withstand the pull. He felt his fingernails drag along the rough bark.

With his eyes wide in horror, he watched as he fell away from the log. He landed on his backpack. He teetered there, afloat like a turtle on his back. He balanced in the water, looking for salvation. Then he toppled over into the familiar wet coldness of the river.

Chapter 114

President Riley called a meeting in the Oval Office. His closest advisors were present as well as the appropriate parties.

He began, "You have all been briefed on the news release from the World Health Organization in regard to the new strain of coronavirus. What we need to figure out is if we are responsible for this. Is this the strain that we created in our labs? Is this what we feared was released?"

Everyone was silent. Some had obvious fear on their faces. Others had their gaze toward the floor. Nobody was speaking.

Impatiently the President began shouting, "WELL, DON'T ALL GO SPEAKING AT ONCE! WE HAVE A SERIOUSE PROBLEM ON OUR HANDS HERE! WHAT DO WE KNOW AND WHAT ARE WE GOING TO DO?"

"Well, we don't know for sure if this is the same case or strain," Dr. Shu-Medley began. "It does appear to be directly related, but we can not be sure without access to the patients or their records."

"Ok, well how hard can that be," asked the President?

"Well Sir, so far, all of the reported cases are in foreign lands. To obtain the information or access would require the cooperation of foreign governments. Thus we would be exposing our position and possible responsibility," Donovan answered.

The President had relied on Donovan's levelheaded advice for many years. They met in Harvard Law School and the President had employed his services ever since.

The President then asked, "Well, can anyone explain how this strain made it to India without rearing its head here in the states?"

"Many of our scientists are from India. It is common for them to travel home frequently to visit family. There are literally thousands of possibilities," Dr. Shu-Medley answered.

Donovan interjected, "Couldn't we obtain the strain specifics from WHO under the guise of offering our assistance or desire to compare with strains in the US?"

The President liked the sound of this and saw that everyone in the room concurred.

"Ok, let's do that. But I also want to find a subject in the US that we can study. We need to nip this in the butt before it becomes a problem. If we can fix this, develop a cure or something, then we can spin this so that we come out on top as heroes," the President instructed.

"Sir, you should know that jurisdictions around the country are inundated with crimes involving missing pets, children, and loved ones. Many of these have turned up with signs of being eaten by humans. The Agency is not able to provide enough assistance. There is even talk of cemeteries that have had bodies removed," Doug Parson, the FBI Director informed.

The room fell silent. The President had a look of horror on his face.

"Ok, we need to move on this. It sounds like this is already blowing up in our faces. If we can confirm that this is our creation, then we will need to make the announcement right away," the President informed. "Doug, what do you need?"

"I need more man power," Doug replied.

"Ok, I can give you access to support from the National Guard, but I don't want panic on the streets. So let's keep it under wraps. The Guard will be ready for deployment as needed to maintain order. I do not want this to turn into a police state, do you understand?"

"Yes Sir. What do you think of enacting a nationwide curfew? We could then use the National Guard at night. The days would be left to the local authorities."

"Do you think that we are to that point? Do we need to enact a curfew? This will surely be cause for alarm and cause paranoia."

"Sir, I do not think that we are to that point as of yet, but do we want to wait until it becomes that bad?"

The President turned his gaze to Donovan, " What do you think?"

"Mr. President, I agree that a curfew will cause panic. I also agree with Mr. Parson, that we need to consider the idea and have it ready to deploy at a moments notice."

"Ok, here's what we will do. Identify the problem areas. Get the Guard mobilized and ready to go. I want them in the areas when we issue the curfew mandate. We will only issue curfews to the identified areas of problem, and we must provide military support.

Understood?"

"Yes Sir."

Chapter 115

The instant freezing cold water on his chest caused Malcolm to involuntarily gasped for air. This caused him to swallow several mouthfuls of ice-cold water. His lungs burned from the freezing temperature.

He rolled over onto his belly and began swimming with every ounce in his body. He knew that every second counted. He had to get out of the river and begin warming up immediately.

Arm over arm, no chance to think, he acted solely on instinct. Kicking with all his might, it was difficult to raise his feet with the weight of his boots that were now filled with water.

With each stroke, he spit at the cold water before gasping for air. His lungs had contracted, making it impossible to obtain the amount of oxygen he needed.

He reached the shore and continued swimming until his chest was clear. Then he began crawling, dragging his legs behind him. He forced his feet into the snowy bank. After gaining his footing, he fully removed his bag and tossed it up on the bank that was now, just above his head.

He methodically placed his feet into the icy bank and quickly moved his way up to safety. He fought his body's desire to convulse, but could not prevent the persistent coughing and gasping for air.

Upon reaching the top of the embankment, Malcolm sprawled out in the snow. He thought how strange it was that the snow felt warm. He tried to catch his breath while he continued to cough up water.

He noticed that his body was not shivering, and that the wet-coldness of his clinging clothes were somehow not bothersome. He was somehow content to just lie there.

Get up. Get UP! GET UP! GEEEETT UUUUPPPP! He demanded to himself.

He knew the signs of hypothermia, and he was now entering the point of no return. After the body stops shivering, it begins to feel warm. It is not unlikely for subjects to be found by searchers by following their trails of clothing that they stripped off. The subjects are usually found naked and dead. He always found it so strange how the mind worked in this way.

No time to contemplate the workings of the human mind now. GET MOVING!

Malcolm forced himself out of his cold-coma. He willed himself to roll over onto his belly. He pumped out 8 push-ups before collapsing in exhaustion. He crawled his legs up under himself into a child's pose. Then he gathered his willpower and cheered himself to a standing position. He yanked and pulled at his clothes with his numbed fingers. He felt like an old man whose gnarled fingers had become useless against the buttons and snaps that had him imprisoned.

Frustrated, he resolved to clawing his jacket and shirts off, over his head. He kicked off his boots and pants. Standing naked on his pile of clothes, he hastily began performing jumping jacks.

No longer able to continue jumping, Malcolm began digging through his bag. Luckily his backpack had protected the contents from becoming wet. He yanked out his Big Agnes down sleeping bag, and wrapped it around his torso like a shawl.

He forced a pair of dry wool socks over his pink feet. He then secured miscellaneous articles of dry clothing around his feet, insulating them from the snow.

Then he pulled out a strip of jerky and began chewing, hoping that the fuel would be enough to stoke his internal flame.

Next, he set about gathering fuel for a fire. He knew that he was knocking on death's door and time was of the essence. He found a fallen tree and began clearing away the snow from the log. He piled up pine needles and dead grass next to the log, that he gathered from a small tree well. Then he pulled off chunks of bark from the fallen tree and propped them up against the tree, over his pile of kindling. Next, he pulled a section of duct tape off of his Nalgene bottle and buried the wadded up section beneath his kindling. He got the sparks from his flashlight to ignite the needles and the tape took off burning.

Malcolm willed his fire to grow. The growing flame instantly improved his mood. His spirits rose with the smoke. The bark and twigs ignited and the fire took to life. The flames began licking at the side of the fallen tree. The crackling lent testimony that the tree was igniting.

Malcolm gathered his belongings and dragged them near the fire. He placed each of his containers near the flame and began warming the water. He grabbed needles from a Blue Spruce and added them to the water. The Blue Spruce would provide flavor and vitamins.

He stood by the fire, rubbing his skin vigorously beneath the sleeping bag. He continued moving, shifting from one leg to the other. The fire continued to grow. He grabbed one of the containers as it began to steam. He sipped the warm liquid. He could feel the warmth travel down his throat, esophagus, and into his stomach. The warmth radiated throughout his core. His body shivered.

YES! A good sign.

Chapter 116

Sheriff Glasgow received an automated phone call from the Federal Emergency Management Agency (FEMA) located out of Oakland. He recognized the number on the caller ID right away. The area code was 510 indicating that it was from the East Bay, but the digits that followed were all nines. This he knew was FEMA.

The message informed him that the Federal Government would be providing assistance to those areas that were experiencing unprecedented levels of crime.

The Federal Government was prepared to enforce a mandatory curfew in areas experiencing extreme levels of crime. It continued to state that the curfew decision was being left to the local authorities to determine.

Local authorities that required National Guard assistance to enforce the curfew were invited to respond to a specific hotline number.

Sheriff Glasgow listened to the message several times before jotting down the number. He hung up the phone and stared at the number on the page.

He wondered about how bad things were getting. He worried about the safety of his own family. He wondered how his jurisdiction compared with others. He knew his department was taxed. They were burning their candles at both ends and getting nowhere.

As a rule the Sheriff never passed up on Federal Aid. He had three employees who specifically focused on seeking after Federal Grant money. Even so, he worried about pulling resources away from larger cities. As always, the Sheriff considered the lives of the constituents that he was elected to serve and protect.

He picked up the phone and called the Federal number to request the National Guard assistance.

Chapter 117

In 2007, with the economic collapse, James began living full-time at the ranch. He had lost his job as an engineer in Tucson. At the time, he and his wife, Beth, had 3 children: Sandra 9, Andrew 7, and Roger was 5.

By then, the ranch was fully self-sustainable, and the family earned money selling the cows that they raised. James also earned money consulting as an engineer.

The ranch was equipped with solar, wind, and a well by 2009. James added a water tower with a lookout "sniper" position from the top. The tower rose 35 feet and provided a great vantage point to survey and protect the immediate surroundings.

By 2010, James had extended the tunnel system connecting his bunker to the water tower and barn. Both had hidden trap doors providing access to the tunnels.

The family practiced a minimum of once a week with firearms, knives, and various weapons. Once a quarter they ran through mock invasions or catastrophes.

Every member studied their choice of martial art: James practiced Krav Maga, Beth and Sandra took up Jiu Jitsu, Andrew studied Kung Fu/Shotokan Karate, and Roger chose Taekwondo.

Each month, a family member was in charge of teaching the others their form of martial art. The family became well rounded and versed in self-defense.

Every Saturday morning, the family would jog the parameter of the property. This kept the members in shape and allowed James to perform a visual inspection of the fencing.

James was extremely proficient at knife throwing. Beth could consistently hit a tin can off a fence post from 100 yards. The kids were all good at shooting handguns, rifles, shotguns, and in the use of bows and arrows.

James did not believe in the apocalyptic predictions of the world ending in 2012, but he was more than prepared should it have occurred. By 2012, he had amassed a solid compound where he and his family could live and survive for years without assistance from the outside world.

Chapter 118

As soon as the warmth began returning to his body, Malcolm began setting up his wet clothing to be dried. He found long branches that he stuck upright into the snow. From these he draped his wet clothes and gear around the fire. He hoped that they would dry before the evening set in.

As Malcolm thawed next to the roaring fire, his stomach reminded him of how hungry he was. He gathered his fishing pole, secured a piece of jerky on the line, and cast it into the river. He hoped to be as lucky as the last time.

Malcolm returned to the fire. He continued thawing out. He also made the attempt of appeasing his hunger pains by filling his belly with warm water.

He continued to add wood to his fire and finally began to feel warm as the skies darkened. It was then that he realized that he had failed to build a shelter.

Quickly, he built a crude lean-to like he had the day before. He set up his sleeping quarters and then prayed that the weather would continue to cooperate.

Malcolm walked to the river, refilled his containers with water, reeled in his fishing line, and recast it back out again. Disappointedly, he returned to his camp. He added logs to the fire and fell asleep as soon as his head touched-down.

Chapter 119

Jack and Tessy were on their way to the local coffee shop for their traditional Sunday morning coffee and Sunday paper reading. They loved spending the mornings catching up with friends and neighbors.

Jack pushed the button to raise the garage door. He opened the passenger side door to their black Subaru. He held the door open for his wife.

They were both moving slowly today. Between Jack's grocery store episode, the loss of the Munger's girl, and the disappearance of neighborhood pets; the air around them was heavy. Their life had taken on a gloom that they were not able to shake.

Jack brought life to the engine with the half turn of the ignition-key. He pushed in the button on the automatic controls and slid the stick into reverse. As he turned his body to look out the back window, his eyes paused on the worried expression of his wife's face. His heart ached. Not only was he helpless to make things better, he was largely to blame for her current state.

Jack placed his right arm on the back of Tessy's seat. Looking over his shoulder he took his foot off the brake pedal and the vehicle gently rolled out and down the driveway.

Jack resumed the correct position, facing forward in the driver's seat. He raised his hand to the sun-visor and pushed the button on the remote to lower the garage door.

He watched in horror as the door lowered and the depiction of graffiti grew.

Tessy gasped and began to cry as the door came to a rest against the concrete floor. Somebody had used red paint to deface their craftsman styled wood doors.

There in dark running red paint were the letters:
"NZ!"

Below this, they had spelled out the words:
"No Zombies!"

.

Chapter 120

That night, Malcolm had an amazingly realistic dream. The dream was of him on a midnight run:

As he ran, he became extremely hungry. He ran down the middle of, what he thought was Grimmer Blvd. He past the China Town Buffet, McDonalds, Taco Bell, and Togo's restaurants. All of them were closed.

He took a right on Fremont Boulevard. He ran passed Mama Elaina's Pizza, Burger King, Mountain Mike's, and Jack in the Box. Everything was closed. Food was not available anywhere.

He was near exhaustion when he stumbled up to the Beacon Station on the corner of Fremont and Blacow. He made his way up to the double glass doors. All of the lights were on. He could see the hotdogs spinning on top of the greasy rollers, next to the icy machine.

Malcolm pulled and pushed on the doors, but they were locked. He banged on the glass, but nobody was inside.

"What is going on around here?"

He slumped to the ground, his back against the glass. He buried his head into the palms of his head.

"I am so hungry," Malcolm began to sob.

His stomach growled furiously loud. He lowered his arms to hug his belly, attempting to muffle the growling.

As he lowered his hands from his face, he realized the growling was not coming from his stomach. There, four feet from where he sat, was a large German Shepherd, looking just as hungry.

The dog continued to growl a low rumbling menacing vibrato. Malcolm's stomach growled back as if answering and challenging the canine. He covered his stomach, hoping to quiet the sound.

The dog lunged at him. Malcolm rolled to his right, avoiding the dog's pounce. The dog agilely changed directions.

Malcolm jumped to his feet and ran toward the brick wall surrounding the convenience store. As he leapt for the wall, he felt the dog's weight bear down on his back. He crashed to the concrete, his nose and cheek slamming. He tried to get back up as the dog began tugging on his windbreaker.

He rolled over swiftly delivering his left elbow into the ribs of the large beast. He followed the motion with a solid right punch. He heard the cracking of ribs and the dog yelped.

Malcolm jumped to his feet again and ran for the dumpster surround. He reached the large steel gates and yanked at the metal with all of his remaining strength. The door slammed into the head of the dog that was intent on making Malcolm his meal.

Stunned from the door, and having lost his fight, the dog ran off and around the corner of the building. Malcolm chased after the dog, keeping his distance.

He rounded the corner of the store and found the dog laying down between the building and the back fence.

As he approached, the dog let out a warning growl. Malcolm searched his surroundings. He picked up the trashcan near the air and water station. He repeatedly slammed the can on the dog's head. The dog made a last ditched defensive attack, but Malcolm was ready. He swiftly pulled on the air hose and wrapped it around the dog's neck. He yanked on the hose with all his might while planting his knee into the dog's back.

The dog eventually stopped moving. Malcolm looked around. The streets were vacant. He looked down at the dog. Then he pulled the dog into the shadows behind the convenience store and began dismantling his kill. He ate until his heart's content.

When he woke, he could still taste the bloody meat in his mouth. His belly felt full and satisfied. He raised his head off the ground and wiped at the drool dripping from his mouth. He pulled his hand away from his mouth, rubbing the liquid substance between his fingers.

He glanced down at his hand to discover it covered in blood.

He immediately backed up onto his knees to examine himself. He stuck his fingers into his mouth, expecting to find that hunger had forced him to chew off his own tongue. His tongue was intact.

He examined the front of his body. He was covered in caked-on-dried blood and what appeared to be dog fur. He searched for a cut, a scrape, or a sign of damage. Nothing.

Chapter 121

Malcolm wondered if he was still trapped inside a dream as he made his way over the lumpy snow toward the river. He stumbled over his own footprints that had frozen solid through the night.

As he approached the river, he glanced upstream at his previous location. He was reminded of his lack of progress and felt discouraged.

He dropped to his knees. His arms flared out and head turned skyward, he screamed. His scream was part anguish and part exhaustion, but mostly the scream was wrought with frustration.

His scream, directed to the heavens above, he hoped to be heard. That God and his Angels would deliver him from the torment that had become his life. He prayed for deliverance from this nightmare, where he felt scared of himself, confused by the obsession to feed on raw meat.

What am I becoming? What is happening to me? Please, Lord, just let me die. Just take my life – here, now. Send me to Hell where I belong.

He was giving up. He could not continue; out of strength, cold, miserable, and scared.

The skies began to fall upon Malcolm in the form of large snowflakes. His situation had transformed from worse to dire. His heart sank. He now felt completely broken.

Arms still sprawled, and with his head turned skyward, he swayed backward and fell onto his back.

He laid there, willing his soul to cry, but beyond the point of tears. He watched the flakes fall from the sky until his eyes begged to close.

Closing his eyes, the snow began to fall in force, quickly burying Malcolm's bloodied shell.

The only thing that he ever wanted, that he had constantly given chase for in life, was the very last thing he wanted now…

Solitude.

ABOUT THE AUTHOR

Joseph L. Wilder, MPA announces his presence as a published author with Solitude. He lives in the East Bay of San Francisco Bay Area with his wife and children.

This is the first attempt by the author at a work of fiction. He found immense joy in the process and looks forward to continuing the story.

Joseph L. Wilder, MPA graduated with a BS in Economics from California State University, Sacramento. He earned his Masters in Public Administration from the University of Phoenix. He now wonders why he failed to major in English.